THE
GALLOW
GLASS

Also by
Brian Keaney

JACOB'S LADDER

The Promises of Dr Sigmundus

THE HOLLOW PEOPLE

THE
GALLOW
GLASS

BRIAN KEANEY

ORCHARD BOOKS

ORCHARD BOOKS
338 Euston Road, London NW1 3BH
Orchard Books Australia
Level 17/205 Kent St, Sydney, NSW 2000

First published in 2007 by Orchard Books
Text copyright © Brian Keaney 2007

The right of Brian Keaney to be identified as the author
of this work has been asserted by him in accordance with
the Copyright, Designs and Patents Act, 1988.

A CIP catalogue record for this book is
available from the British Library.

ISBN 978 1 84616 087 5 (hardback)
ISBN 978 1 84616 089 9 (paperback)

1 3 5 7 9 10 8 6 4 2

Printed in Great Britain

The paper and board used in this paperback are natural
recyclable products made from wood grown in sustainable
forests. The manufacturing processes conform to the
environmental regulations of the country of origin.

Orchard Books is a division of Hachette Children's Books,
an Hachette Livre UK company

www.orchardbooks.co.uk.

The Gallowglass ar pycked and scelected men of great and mightie bodies, crewell without compassion. The greatest force of the battell consisteth in them, choosing rather to dye than to yeeld.

Philip O'Sullivan-Beare (1621)

Author's Note

Gallowglass was the name given to a group of mercenary soldiers who took part in the wars in Scotland and Ireland in the thirteenth, fourteenth and fifteenth centuries. They were extremely efficient at their job, terrifying the opposition, and could perhaps be described as the original SAS. Their real name was Gallóglaigh, which is Gaelic for foreign soldiers. But the English found this impossible to pronounce and called them Gallowglass instead.

Brian Keaney
London
July 2007

CONTENTS

PART ONE: THE CALL

PART TWO: THE ANSWER

Part One
THE CALL

THE NECROPOLIS

The sun was setting on the Necropolis, a vast sprawling city of the dead where the inhabitants of Ellison had been buried for over three hundred years. Once, it had been very grand, with rows of headstones that stretched for miles in every direction, huge family vaults and elaborate marble statues. But with the passing of time it had become sadly neglected. Now bird droppings covered its crumbling monuments and its broad avenues were overgrown with trees and bushes.

Beneath one of the larger tombs the ground had subsided to leave a cavernous opening and, as the shadows darkened, a figure began to crawl from this hole. Filthy, bedraggled, and half-starved, it looked like an animal creeping stealthily from its lair. But it was Dante Cazabon.

Dazed and bewildered by the effort of overcoming the creature that had once been Doctor Sigmundus, he had fled from the Star Chamber. For weeks he had wandered the outskirts of the city looking for somewhere to hide. He had outwitted soldiers and security guards, sleeping in sheds and barns, moving from place to place like a beggar. Finally, he had come to the Necropolis, and made it his refuge.

Now he scrabbled about on the ground, searching for something to eat. It was days since food had passed his lips and he knew that he would soon be too weak to do anything other than lie down and die. And a voice in his head urged him to do just that. It would be so much easier than struggling on. But Dante refused to listen.

Near the entrance to the Necropolis was a decaying two-storey house. He had spent the last two days observing it and had seen several people come and go. Only one of them, an elderly man, seemed to remain inside for any length of time. But even if there were an army within its walls, Dante had made up his mind to break in.

Inside the house Malachy Mazotta, supervisor of the Necropolis, sat in his study, completing entries in the ledger of deaths. On shelves against the wall stood countless earlier volumes. Their pages contained the names of all those whom the Necropolis had swallowed up. A tall man once, he was stooped now from years spent bending over his desk, and his face held a look of permanent disappointment. What remained of his hair was completely white but his mind had lost none of its alertness. As he wrote, he gradually became aware of noises coming from the kitchen. The rats were getting bolder, he told himself.

Rats and corpses were his constant companions and he kept a shotgun standing ready in case either of them should pluck up the courage to turn on him. Silently, he got up from his chair and made his way across the room.

He slipped off the shotgun's safety catch, then kicked open the kitchen door.

In the middle of the room stood a wild-looking teenager, tearing at a loaf of bread with his teeth. Malachy raised the shotgun. 'Don't move!' he warned.

Dante stared back at him.

'What do you think you're doing, breaking into my house and stealing my food?' Malachy continued.

Suddenly the doorbell rang.

Malachy made no move to answer. 'That's my assistant, Kurt,' he told Dante, speaking softly. 'He's big and strong and very keen on his work. What do you think will happen if he finds out about you?'

'I don't know,' Dante replied.

'He'll insist that I inform the authorities in Ellison. If not, he'll do so himself. So I'm going to give you a choice. You can agree to answer my questions. And then we'll see what happens next. Or I can tell Kurt about you right now and the situation will be out of my hands. Which is it to be?'

'I'll answer your questions,' Dante said.

'Good.' Malachy pointed his shotgun at a door in a corner of the kitchen. 'Inside!'

Dante opened the door and saw that it led to a narrow pantry, lined with shelves from floor to ceiling. He stepped inside and the door was locked behind him. Then the old man's footsteps retreated from the kitchen. While Dante waited in the darkness, he continued to devour the loaf of bread.

After some time the door of the pantry opened again

13

and Malachy ordered Dante out into the kitchen once more. 'Kurt has gone home,' he said. 'Now you must keep your side of the bargain and tell me about yourself.'

'Can I have something to drink first?' Dante asked.

Malachy nodded reluctantly. Still holding the shotgun in one hand, he pointed to the tap by the sink. 'There's a mug over there,' he said. 'Help yourself.'

Dante filled the mug with water and drank deeply. 'May I sit down?' he asked.

'If you must.'

After so long without food, eating had exhausted him. Dante would have liked to put his head on the table and go to sleep. But the old man was waiting.

'It's not a simple story,' Dante began. 'To be honest, I'm not sure I understand it all, myself.'

'Perhaps not,' Malachy agreed, 'but I would guess that your tale begins with you realising that Ichor has no effect on you. Am I right?'

'How did you know that?' Dante demanded warily.

'That's easy enough. Breaking into my kitchen was a criminal act. Only those who aren't affected by Ichor would consider such behaviour.'

Realisation dawned on Dante. 'It doesn't work on you either, does it?' he asked.

Malachy merely raised one eyebrow. 'I'm asking the questions,' he declared.

Dante was convinced that he was right and felt sufficiently emboldened to tell at least part of his story. 'My name is Dante Cazabon,' he began. 'I used to be a kitchen boy in the asylum of Tarnagar. Have you heard of it?'

Malachy nodded.

'I never knew my father. All I was told about my mother was that she was an inmate in the asylum and that she killed herself when I was a baby. And this was what I believed until one day a patient called Ezekiel Semiramis arrived.'

A look of interest came over the old man's face.

'Do you know him?' Dante asked.

'I have heard the name,' Malachy admitted. 'And a handful of rumours that sound too far-fetched to be true. Carry on with your story.'

Dante described how Ezekiel Semiramis had told him that his mother had been murdered and that he himself had known her in the ruined city of Moiteera. 'I'd never heard of such a place before,' he continued, 'but there was a girl called Bea on the island who hadn't yet come of age. She told me that she often dreamt of a ruined city.'

He expected the old man to look shocked at the mention of dreaming, a forbidden topic in Gehenna, but Malachy seemed unperturbed.

'I wanted to ask Ezekiel more about my mother,' Dante went on, 'but I was forbidden to communicate with him and when I tried to do so secretly, I was caught and locked up. I expected to spend the rest of my days in a cell but Ezekiel rescued me, and my friend Bea. He took us to Moiteera and we lived there for three months until one day we were attacked by soldiers. In the battle, Bea was injured and we had no choice but to bring her to a hospital for treatment. That was how I was recaptured. They brought me to Ellison but once again I escaped. Since that time I have wandered about, sleeping rough, eating whatever I could find until I made my way here.'

'And what do you plan to do next?' Malachy asked.

'I promised I would return for Bea and when I have the strength, that's what I will do, though I've no idea where to look for her.'

The old man looked thoughtful. 'You haven't told me everything,' he said. 'That's obvious. But it's enough for the time being. There's a great deal for me to think about. In the meantime, what am I going to do with you?'

Dante looked anxiously at him.

'You can stay here tonight, but only on one condition.'

'What's that?'

'You must take a bath. You stink like a dead dog.'

THE MIDDLE OF NOWHERE

'Why don't you just admit it? We're lost,' Nyro said.

Luther shook his head and carried on studying the map. 'We just took a couple of wrong turnings a few miles back, that's all. We can work out where we are now.'

'We're in the middle of nowhere,' Nyro told him. 'Just take a look around you.'

It was true. The track the two teenage boys had been following for most of the afternoon had finally petered out. Ahead was a dense plantation of fir trees. Behind them stretched open moorland as far as the eye could see.

When they had started out two days ago, the idea of spending a few days hiking through the wilderness that lay between Tavor and its neighbour, Gehenna, had seemed a really good one. Now they were not so sure. 'Maybe we should turn round and go back the way we came,' Nyro said. 'At least we'll know where we're going.'

Luther shook his head. 'We can't do that. It'll be dark soon.'

'So what do you suggest?'

Luther frowned and went back to studying the map. He was the taller of the two and the older, though only by a few months. Well-built and athletic, his face was already beginning to assume the features he would wear as an adult.

Nyro, on the other hand, still looked like a boy. He had soft brown hair that was always falling over his eyes and he had a baby-face that looked even younger when he was anxious, as he was now.

Luther looked up at him and smiled reassuringly. 'I know where we are.' He held out the map and pointed with his finger. 'We're just here. We need to cut through this belt of trees and pick up the road on the other side.'

Nyro looked sceptical. 'You're suggesting we head off into the forest?'

'It's not a forest, it's just a narrow strip of woodland. There's a bit of open country on the other side and then we hit the road.'

'Supposing we get lost?'

Luther folded the map and put it in his rucksack. 'We're already lost,' he said. 'Come on, it's going to be all right.'

Shouldering his rucksack, he set off between the trees. Nyro hesitated, then followed. Ever since they had been little boys he'd been following Luther. And usually, he'd felt perfectly happy about it. But for the last hour he'd had an uneasy feeling that something was going to go wrong and the feeling was getting stronger with every passing moment. What if night fell and they hadn't found their way out of the wood? They could wander around all night getting more and more lost.

But it was soon clear that Luther had been right

about the wood. The trees rapidly began to thin out and Nyro was just beginning to think that he had been worrying about nothing when they found themselves confronted by a chain-link fence about three metres high, stretching as far as they could see in either direction. On the other side of the fence was a huge field of tall purple flowers.

'What's this?' Nyro asked.

Luther shook his head. 'I don't know. It wasn't on the map. But there's only one way over it.'

'You're not suggesting we climb it?' Nyro asked.

'Why not?'

'Because it's been put there to keep people out. This is obviously private land.'

'I don't care. I'm not turning back,' Luther told him. 'I'm going to cross that field.' He put his hands on the fence and began to climb. Nyro watched as his friend hauled himself up, balanced precariously at the top for a moment, then began climbing down the other side. 'See!' he said, when he reached the ground on the other side. 'It's easy. Come on.'

Nyro took hold of the fence and began to climb. But the rucksack on his back made it hard to keep his balance and he wobbled alarmingly as he reached the top. Steadying himself, he began climbing down the other side.

Just then a breeze sprang up and the whole field rippled hypnotically. There was something strangely evocative about it, like a landscape glimpsed in a dream.

'Those flowers are so bright,' Luther said. 'As if they

were electric. Have you ever seen anything like them before?'

But Nyro didn't answer. The truth was that he didn't feel much like talking. A feeling had been growing in his mind ever since he'd first seen those flowers, an awareness that he was just a tiny speck in the middle of a vast universe, that he really didn't matter at all. 'Or is it that I matter very much?' he asked himself. For some reason, he couldn't make up his mind which was correct. Perhaps it was both. Yes, that was it. He didn't really matter and he mattered very much. He suddenly understood that something could be true and its opposite could be true at exactly the same time. 'At this particular moment,' he told himself, 'I am the most important point in the entire universe and also, no more than a tiny speck. How is it that I've never realised this before?'

'I'm going to take a closer look,' Luther said.

Slowly the meaning of Luther's words began to sink in and very faintly an alarm bell began ringing in the back of Nyro's mind. There was something about those plants that was like going too near a very hot fire. When you approached a fire, the heat was a warning that you should stop and turn back, or you might be badly burned – burned to death even. And somehow the colour of those blooms seemed to be the same sort of warning.

'But they're only flowers,' he told himself.

So why did the atmosphere around them seem to be charged with energy, like the air shimmering above the road on a hot summer's day?

'Luther!' he called out. 'I'm not sure that's such a good idea.'

But his friend was already standing among the flowers and, as Nyro watched, Luther put his face right up against the bright purple petals, breathing in their rich fragrance. Suddenly he straightened up and staggered backwards. He opened his mouth, as if to say something, then collapsed onto the ground.

Panic-stricken, Nyro ran towards him. But the closer he got, the more he seemed to be moving in slow-motion, as if wading through water. When he finally reached Luther, he bent down and shook him but there was no response. He could feel the scent of the flowers making him light-headed and dizzy and he knew it would be a mistake to stay there any longer. So, taking hold of his friend's legs, he dragged him as far from the field as possible. Then he knelt down on the ground and tried again to wake him.

Luther did not even appear to be breathing. Nyro struggled to remember what he had learned about artificial respiration. But that sweet, intoxicating fragrance was still filling his head, like smoke in a crowded room.

As he stood there, his mind in chaos, he heard the sound of an engine growing gradually louder. A jeep drove along the track at the edge of the field. When he waved his arms frantically, it screeched to a halt and two soldiers jumped out, their radios crackling. Both were wearing what looked like gas masks. One of them held a rifle pointed at Nyro.

'Hands on your head!' he ordered.

'Something's happened to my friend,' Nyro told him. 'I don't think he's breathing.'

'I said, hands on your head!'

'He needs a doctor!' Nyro protested.

'Shut up!'

The second soldier took a bag from the back of the jeep and bent down over Luther. He unzipped Luther's jacket and took hold of his T-shirt with both hands. Quickly and efficiently he ripped it open, then took a syringe out of his bag. He loaded it carefully, paused for a moment, then jammed the needle into Luther's chest. Luther's eyes jerked open and he began coughing.

'Into the jeep!' the other soldier told Nyro.

'But will my friend be all right?'

The soldier pointed his rifle directly at Nyro's head. 'Just get in the jeep!' he ordered.

Nyro did as he was told. The soldier got into the driver's seat and started the engine. Then they drove off without another word, leaving Luther still lying on the ground with the soldier standing beside him, talking rapidly into his radio.

MIST

Dante stood in the gloom of a darkened room. Where was he? He had no idea. But he could hear breathing. There was someone sleeping in the bed against the wall. Cautiously, he crept towards the figure and peered at its face. With a shock, he stepped backwards again. The figure in the bed was himself!

Instantly, he knew that he was in between waking and sleeping and had left his physical body behind. This other body was simply an extension of his mind. He could use it to travel from one place to another, just by thinking about it. That was how he had found Bea when she had been lost Moiteera. 'Maybe I can find her again,' he told himself.

But before he could do so, his attention was seized by a small grey door that had suddenly appeared in the middle of the room. It seemed to be floating by itself. Taking a step closer, he saw that the surface of the door was covered in symbols. Even though he did not understand the meaning of the individual shapes, and even though they changed as he looked at them, the message was somehow entirely clear.

Open the door, Dante, and step inside.

He had seen this door once before when he had

confronted the creature that had taken possession of Doctor Sigmundus. On that occasion he had resisted the invitation, believing that he was not yet ready. This time he was determined to discover its secrets. He took hold of the handle and the door swung open. The doorway was filled with mist. Dante hesitated for just a second, then stepped through.

He was in a high-ceilinged room. Its walls were lined with books and, seated at a long table in the centre, were a man and woman, both smiling as though they were expecting him.

'Welcome, Dante,' the woman said, giving him a look that was full of tenderness. Something about her voice was instantly familiar. Then he remembered! It was the same voice he had heard whispering to him in the Star Chamber, telling him that he could walk away from there and that no one could stop him.

'Mother, is that you?' he asked, hardly daring to believe it could be true.

Yashar Cazabon nodded. 'Yes, of course.'

He wanted to rush over and put his arms around her – but she shook her head sadly. 'You will not be able to touch me, I'm afraid. I'm not really here at all.'

'Neither of us is,' added her companion, and now Dante recognised his father, Alvar Mendini, from the statue that had stood in the centre of Moiteera.

'I think the sculptor flattered me a little,' his father said, reading his son's mind. 'But I rather like his impression of me, so I decided to use it.' His voice was deep and resonant and his eyes twinkled with mischievous humour.

'Am I dead, too?' Dante asked.

His mother shook her head. 'You are merely between life and death, Dante. Soon you must return to the land of the living, for you have a great deal of work to do there.'

'What sort of work?'

'The thing that has taken over Sigmundus' body must be finally defeated.'

'It is a creature from the depths of the Odyll,' his father explained. 'It uses the name "Orobas".' As he said this, the room seemed to shudder and distort, and Dante's head filled with a painful buzzing.

'Even to speak its name is to draw some part of its attention,' his father told him.

'What does it want?'

'The Odyll is a realm of pure energy,' his mother continued, 'and those that inhabit it are nothing but energy and will; yet many of them were once flesh and blood and long to experience the material world once more. That is why this creature has possessed Sigmundus and many more before him. It is why it desires, more than anything, to remain in your world. But as the body it inhabits becomes older, its hold on mortal life grows more tenuous. It would like to take possession of you, and if it can find a way, that is precisely what it will do. At the same time, however, its appetite for the mortal world is increasing. Indeed, life alone is not enough for it. It wants power.'

'But it already controls Gehenna completely,' Dante pointed out.

'Gehenna is just the beginning,' his father said. 'It intends to spread its dominion across the entire world.'

'And for that purpose it is trying to create a new kind of warrior,' his mother continued, 'one whose senses will be much greater than those of other human beings. Only you can stop this happening.'

'Why me?' Dante demanded. 'In the Star Chamber the creature felt so much stronger than me. You know that. I only survived with your help.' He shook his head. 'I'm not the force that everyone thinks I am.'

'Dante, look into this bowl,' his father told him.

There was a shallow blue bowl filled with water in the centre of the table. As Dante gazed at the surface of the water, ripples spread across it, then stilled. Reflected in its surface, Dante saw a boy, about eight or nine years of age, standing beside a tree. He recognised the location as the woods surrounding Tarnagar and the boy he was watching as himself.

The boy was crouching down carefully, trying to make as little noise as possible. 'What was I staring at so intently?' Dante asked himself. Of course! With this remembrance a transformation came over him. He became his younger self once more, crouching silently in the woods of Tarnagar staring in terrified fascination at something that looked like a man – except that it was at least eight feet tall and had wings on its back. The creature was standing perfectly still amid the trees with its head a little to one side, as if listening.

Suddenly a bird flew low between the trees, diverting Dante's attention. In that split second the winged figure vanished. There was only a twisted old tree in its place. Had it merely been his imagination playing tricks with the shadows? He picked up a broken branch from the ground, walked over to the twisted tree and struck it as hard as he could. The branch broke in half and Dante walked away in disgust.

The picture in the bowl faded and the older Dante looked up at his father once more. 'Was there really a winged man?' he asked.

Alvar nodded. 'Tzavinyah watches over you at all times.'

'But who is he?'

'Tzavinyah is the messenger of the Odyll,' his mother told him. 'It is a truly remarkable thing that he chose to show himself to you. It is even more remarkable that you were able to see him.'

'But only for an instant,' Dante pointed out.

'Everything that has ever been and everything that ever will be happens in an instant,' she replied.

As she spoke, the room began to fill with mist and Dante sensed that the meeting was coming to an end.

'Wait!' he said. 'Can you tell me where my friend Bea is?'

'You must search for her in Barzach,' Yashar told him.

'Where is that?' Dante asked.

But the grey tide was all around him now, paralysing his body and numbing his mind. He could see his mother's lips moving but he could hear nothing of what she said. Then the mist entered his mind completely, and even the sight of her was washed away.

When he came to, he was lying in a strange bed in a room he did not recognise and someone was knocking loudly on the door.

'Who is it?' Dante called out.

'It's me, of course. Who else?' The door opened and Malachy Mazotta stood in the doorway.

Dante sat up in bed, blinking in confusion.

'It's time to get up,' Malachy told him. 'You'll find some clean clothes in the bottom of that chest.'

'Have you decided what you're going to do with me?' Dante asked.

The old man shook his head. 'That depends upon you,' he said. 'Hurry up and get dressed. Kurt will be here in an hour.'

Over breakfast Malachy asked Dante about his plans. 'If I were to let you walk out of here right now, where would you go?' he demanded.

'To a place called Barzach,' Dante told him.

Malachy frowned. 'Why Barzach?'

'I had a dream in which someone told me my friend was there, though I've no idea how to find the place.'

Malachy was silent for a long time. 'Everything happens for a reason,' he said at last. 'That was what my wife used to tell me. I always said it was nonsense. But these days I'm not so sure. Anyway, I've made up my mind. I'm going to help you.'

'Thank you.'

'Now, listen carefully. If someone dies on the outskirts of the city, it's my responsibility to collect the remains. I normally send Kurt. But this morning I'm going to tell him I have received a call. I will take the hearse and you will come with me – in the coffin.'

'But where are we going?' Dante asked.

'To Barzach, of course. Where else?'

MOONLIGHT

The jeep drew up outside a low brick building. Nyro was marched inside and taken to a small, rather overcrowded room where a red-faced officer in a peaked cap sat behind a desk, talking on the telephone. He looked up irritably as they entered.

'Yes, of course I realise the gravity of the situation,' he was saying. 'Look, the boy is here now. I'll call you back.' He put down the phone and glared at Nyro. 'Sit down!' he barked.

Nyro sat.

'You can go now, Corporal Jenkins,' the officer continued. 'Wait outside.'

The officer turned his full attention to Nyro. 'My name is Brigadier Giddings,' he announced. 'And you are?'

'Nyro Balash.'

'Address?'

Nyro gave his address.

'Good. Now then, what were you doing in the field?'

'We were trying to get to the other side.'

'Don't try to be smart with me, young man!'

'It's the truth! Look, I'm not saying anything else until you tell me what's happened to Luther.'

Brigadier Giddings sighed. 'Your friend had some

sort of seizure,' he said. 'At the moment he is receiving medical attention. He'll be perfectly all right in a couple of hours. Now, who told you where to find the field?'

'Nobody told us. We discovered it by accident.'

The interview went on for a very long time. Over and over again, Nyro assured the brigadier that their discovery of the flowers had been accidental but he seemed convinced that the two boys had been deliberately spying. He made Nyro describe everything he had felt after coming across the flowers. He insisted on hearing it all in the minutest detail, which wasn't easy because some of the facts had become blurred in Nyro's mind. Finally, he seemed to accept Nyro's story. Corporal Jenkins, now minus his face mask, was summoned back into the office to take Nyro to another part of the building where a white-coated doctor gave him a medical examination.

When this was over he was led back outside. It was dark now and the sky was ablaze with stars. Nyro was ordered into the back of a truck where he sat on a bench with the stony-faced corporal. Shortly afterwards, Luther clambered in and sat down opposite them. At first Nyro felt a huge sense of relief at his friend's appearance. But Luther looked terrible. His face was ghostly white, there were dark shadows under his eyes and he moved like a sleepwalker. Behind him came Brigadier Giddings. Once the doors of the truck were closed, the engine started up and they were driven off without another word.

They arrived at Nyro's home in the early hours of the morning. Brigadier Giddings had no compunction about waking Nyro's parents, while Luther waited in the truck under the watchful eye of Corporal Jenkins. The Brigadier informed Nyro's mother and father that their son had been trespassing on government property, that the decision had been taken not to prosecute him on this occasion but that, should there be any further incidents, the consequences would be severe.

'However, assuming that Nyro gives us no further trouble,' Brigadier Giddings continued, 'we are prepared to forget the whole thing. In return we expect Nyro and yourselves to do the same. And when I say forget, I mean wipe the incident from your mind completely. Nyro will never mention anything that he has done, seen or heard this weekend. Is that perfectly clear?'

They nodded.

'Good.' The Brigadier opened his briefcase and took out some papers. 'I've brought along a document for you to sign. It clearly states that any conversation you have had with me in respect of the behaviour of your son during this weekend is to be regarded as an official state secret and is therefore covered by the State Secrets Act. In case you are not aware, the penalty for breaking this act is up to twenty-five years in prison. Read the document and sign at the bottom.'

White-faced, Nyro's parents quickly scanned the document and signed.

The Brigadier put it in his briefcase and left.

Nyro didn't even try explaining to his parents what had really happened. The Brigadier had done his job thoroughly and they were too scared to discuss the matter.

On the following Monday morning Nyro got to school early and stood inside the gates, waiting anxiously for Luther to appear. Finally, the bell rang and he was forced to go inside with the other students.

To Nyro's surprise, they had a new teacher, a young woman called Miss Bukowski. She took the register without calling Luther's name. As they were getting ready to go to their first lesson, Nyro went up to her.

'Excuse me, miss.'

'Yes?'

'I think you missed someone off the register – Luther Vavohu.'

Miss Bukowski frowned, opened the register and checked through the list of names.

'There's no one of that name down here.'

'But he was in this class last term,' Nyro protested.

Miss Bukowski shrugged. 'Perhaps you should ask in the office. Now you'd better hurry up or you'll be late for your first class.'

It was lunchtime before Nyro got a chance to go to the school office and ask about Luther.

'I don't believe there's anyone of that name on the school roll,' the secretary told him.

'Yes there is,' Nyro assured her. 'He was in the same class as me last term.'

She shook her head. 'You must be mistaken,' she said. 'We have no records for a Luther Vavohu.'

'That's ridiculous!' protested. 'He was in my class just a few weeks ago. Can't you just look him up?'

'I've already told you that you've made a mistake,'

the secretary replied. 'There has never been a Luther Vavohu at this school. Now if you don't mind, I've got a great deal of work to do.'

Nyro was turning away in frustration when he saw a tall blond-haired boy called Aaron who had regularly played football with himself and Luther. 'Hey Aaron,' Nyro said. 'Could you just help me sort something out with the secretary?'

'Sure,' Aaron said. 'What's the problem?'

'I'm trying to find out whether Luther has been transferred to another class and she doesn't even seem to have any records for him.'

'Luther who?' Aaron asked.

Nyro looked at him in amazement. 'Luther who you played football with all last term.'

Aaron looked puzzled. 'I don't remember any Luther.'

'Is this some kind of a joke?' Nyro demanded.

Aaron shrugged. 'You tell me,' he said.

It was the same story with everyone Nyro asked, students and teachers alike. No one could remember anything at all about a boy called Luther Vavohu.

When school was over, Nyro phoned Luther's house. The line was out of order and it stayed that way for the rest of the week. On Friday night Nyro decided to go over there. His parents had gone out to celebrate their wedding anniversary so there were no awkward questions. All the same, he felt a little nervous about the visit – what if the authorities were watching?

He had just turned into Luther's road when he saw his friend coming out of the house, walking along the road in the opposite direction. Nyro's first instinct was to call out, but he hesitated. There was something odd about the way Luther was moving, bending low and loping along almost like some kind of animal. Without really knowing why, Nyro decided to follow him.

Luther threaded his way through the back streets, towards the outskirts of the city. From time to time Nyro got the feeling that his friend knew he was being followed but, if so, he gave no sign.

At last he reached Liminal Park, the city's largest open space, stretching in a great arc around the northern suburbs. At this time of night the park was closed, but Luther simply put a hand on the railings and leapt over. Nyro shook his head, astonished at his friend's agility. When he reached the railings himself moments later, he struggled to climb over.

The park was laid out on rising ground and it soon became clear that Luther was heading for the highest point. Tirelessly, he climbed until he stood at the top, as still as a statue, his silhouette outlined against the night sky. A little lower down the slope, Nyro halted, waiting to see what would happen next.

For a long time Luther remained completely motionless. Suddenly the moon came out from behind the clouds. Immediately, he raised his arms above his head, as if in greeting. Then he put his head back and howled, an unearthly sound that turned Nyro's blood to ice.

THE NAKARA

A freight train rumbled along the line that ran from Ellison to the mountain towns of the Ichor Belt, an area in northwestern Gehenna where the drug that kept the whole country under control was mined and processed. As the first few flakes of snow began to drift down from the night sky, a signal changed to red and the train screeched to a halt. Unnoticed, three hooded figures jumped down from one of the carriages and crouched behind the bushes until the train had moved on.

'The entrance to the sewer is less than a mile from here,' said one of the three, a well-built young man with a scar on his forehead. 'Once we're inside, It's straight ahead, then first right, second left, straight ahead again and the first ladder you see brings you up into the middle of the compound.'

The young man was called Albigen and he was a member of the Púca, a band of fighters who were determined to destroy the rule of Doctor Sigmundus. It was their leader, Ezekiel Semiramis, who had rescued Dante from the asylum on Tarnagar. Now Ezekiel himself spoke. 'Remember, if anything goes wrong after this point we split up and each of us makes his own way back.'

The other two nodded.

Ezekiel shifted the rucksack on his back, grimacing as he did so. 'Let's get going.'

'Do you want me to carry your pack for a little while?' Albigen asked.

Ezekiel shook his head. 'I'm fine,' he replied.

'You're not fine,' the third member of the group, a red-haired girl named Maeve, told him. 'It's obvious that you haven't fully recovered from the infection you got after the wound in your arm. You should have left this mission to Albigen and me'

'I've told you, I'm perfectly all right,' Ezekiel insisted. 'Now no more talking unless it's absolutely necessary.'

The three of them made their way in silence over the scrubland which bordered the railway. After some time Albigen stopped in front of a large metal drain cover.

'This is it!'

He and Maeve each took hold of one end of the drain cover and lifted it up to reveal a square shaft. A metal ladder was set into the side and with Albigen leading the way, they began their descent into the sewer. A short while later they re-emerged in a concrete yard between anonymous industrial buildings. The area was only partially illuminated by overhead lighting and they crouched down in the shadows behind some refuse bins.

Albigen pointed out a low brick building on the other side of the compound. 'That's the electricity generator,' he told them.

'I don't see any guards,' Ezekiel observed.

'No. Only the building at the eastern end of the

compound is guarded. Perhaps that's where most of the Ichor processing is going on at the moment – I'm not sure. But it doesn't matter to us where their activities are concentrated. If we blow up the generator we paralyse the entire operation.'

'Then let's get started,' Ezekiel said. 'Albigen, you and I will place the explosives at the key points. Maeve, you run the fuse wire back to here.'

They made their way over to the building in which the generator was housed. They had rehearsed the procedure thoroughly and were soon finished, ready to set off the charge. But as they crouched down beside the refuse bins, they heard talking and a burst of laughter. A group of young women were coming out of the brightly lit building at the eastern end of the compound.

'Wait until they're gone,' Ezekiel whispered. 'We don't want to run the risk of anyone getting injured by flying debris.'

The group of women continued to make their way across the compound, chatting as they went.

'They look like nurses,' Maeve observed.

'What are nurses doing in an Ichor processing plant?' Ezekiel mused.

'Maybe that part of the building is a hospital wing,' Albigen suggested.

Ezekiel frowned. 'If that's the case, then we can't destroy the power supply for the entire complex,' he said. 'People's lives might depend on electrical equipment continuing to function.'

'But this operation has taken weeks of surveillance

and planning,' Albigen objected. 'We can't just throw all that away because we've seen a group of nurses. They might be visiting, or something. Let's go and take a closer look at that building.'

'Good idea,' Ezekiel agreed. 'But please be extra careful. I've already lost Dante and Bea, remember.'

They got as close as they dared and studied the guards for some time. There were two at the front entrance and two more at the rear. Once every ten minutes one of the front guards patrolled the left hand side of the building while a rear guard patrolled the right hand side.

'The level of security is far too high for a hospital,' Ezekiel said after a while. 'We're going to have to get inside the building if we want to find out what's really going on. I could summon odyllic force, but...' He hesitated.

'You don't know who or what is in there,' Albigen pointed out. 'It might not be wise.' The truth was, he wasn't convinced that Ezekiel, in his weakened state, was up to the task of entering the odyllic world, but he didn't like to say so.

'Listen,' Maeve said, 'it takes the guards just over four minutes to get all the way round the building, right? Which means there are six minutes when either side of the building is vulnerable. I saw an open fanlight half way down on the left hand side.'

'Yes, but it's too small,' Ezekiel objected.

'I think I could get through.'

'What if you get stuck? There isn't enough time.'

'I can hide beside those packing crates near the building. As soon as the guard disappears round the corner, I'll run up to the window, get up on the ledge and climb through the fanlight. A minute to get to the building, maybe five minutes to get through. I'll be fine. Besides, what other choice have we got?'

Ezekiel hesitated. Finally, he nodded. 'We'll try it. But I'll come with you. Once you're inside, open the window and let me in. Albigen, go back to the refuse bins and wait there. If there's any trouble, get out on your own. But don't set off the charge unless you hear from me. Understand?'

Albigen opened his mouth to protest but a look from the older man silenced him. Reluctantly, he nodded and disappeared into the shadows. Ezekiel and Maeve took up their positions, watching while the guard made his way steadily around the side of the building. As soon as he had turned the corner at the rear, Maeve sprinted to the window. In a flash she had her feet on the sill and began to wriggle through the fanlight. It was a very tight fit and at one point she hung there with half her body inside and her legs waving about. But, to Ezekiel's relief, she finally scrambled through just as the second guard rounded the corner. Maeve waited until he had followed his colleague round the edge of the building. Then she opened the window beneath the fanlight. Ezekiel ran to the building and climbed inside.

They were in a store room with dozens of identical wooden crates lined up against the far wall. Apart from that, the place was empty. The most noticeable thing about the room was a very strong smell, almost like incense.

'What's that scent?' Maeve asked.

'I don't know, but it seems to be coming from these crates,' Ezekiel replied.

'Maybe we should see what's inside them,' Maeve suggested. She started to lift the lid but Ezekiel stopped her.

'Wait!' he said, sharply. 'There's something strange about this. I don't know what it is, but this smell reminds me of something that makes me uneasy.'

He lifted the lid of one of the crates and saw that underneath the thick layers of packaging it was filled with bottles of purple liquid.

'What are they?' Maeve asked.

There were no labels on the bottles. Ezekiel unscrewed the top of one and immediately the smell in the room become much more intense. Maeve found herself growing dizzy and for a moment she lost all sense of who she was.

White-faced and shocked, Ezekiel screwed the lid back on.

'What *is* that stuff?' Maeve asked.

'I can't identify it precisely,' Ezekiel replied. 'But I can tell you what it does. It opens a window in the mind that looks out upon the Nakara.'

'What's the Nakara?'

'The Nakara is the darkest level of the Odyll. Terrible things lurk there. Come on, let's get out of this room and see what else is going on here.'

Cautiously, Ezekiel opened the door and peered outside. At the end of the corridor were a pair of double doors. As he watched, they opened and he ducked back inside, keeping the door slightly ajar. Two nurses came out of the room, wheeling a bed between them. They were wearing masks on their faces. As soon as they were out of sight, Ezekiel and Maeve hurried down the corridor into the room the nurses had just left.

Inside, half a dozen patients lay unconscious on their beds. Each one was connected to a machine which measured their vital signs and regulated a drip filled with purple liquid. Maeve felt herself becoming light-headed once again and she struggled to stay focused.

Ezekiel looked around and shook his head. 'What are they *doing* to these people?' he said.

Just then, one of the patients, a young man not much older than Albigen, opened his eyes and saw Ezekiel standing over him.

'Who are you?' he whispered.

'A friend,' Ezekiel assured him.

'Then kill me,' the young man said. 'I can't stand any more of this.'

Ezekiel shook his head. 'I'm sorry. I cannot do that,' he said.

'Please,' the young man begged, his voice rising in pitch. 'If you have any humanity, kill me. I beg you.'

As Ezekiel gazed down at him in horror, the patient in the next bed opened his eyes and struggled to sit up in the bed. 'And me,' he cried out. 'Kill me, too. Release me from this torture.' The sound of his cries awakened the other patients. One by one, they began clamouring for death, arms outstretched towards Ezekiel and Maeve.

Suddenly, the double doors opened and a nurse stood looking into the ward, her eyes wide with alarm. 'What are you doing here?' she demanded, her voice muffled by her thick mask.

'Quick, through the other entrance!' Ezekiel whispered.

He and Maeve ran down the middle of the ward and through the doors at the other end as the nurse gave chase. Ezekiel pushed a trolley into her path and she stumbled, cursing and rubbing her leg. They darted down another corridor and Ezekiel opened the first door they came across. It led to a small shower room. Quickly, Ezekiel locked the door behind them while Maeve opened the window and put her head outside. 'No sign of the guards,' she said. 'They're probably inside the building, looking for us.'

They climbed out of the window and began running across the compound towards the refuse bins. Soon enough they heard shouting behind them, followed by a gunshot.

Albigen had been waiting with growing anxiety. When he heard the shot, he remembered Ezekiel's orders, but he couldn't bear to abandon his colleagues. Powerful searchlights came on, picking out Ezekiel and Maeve racing across the compound. At any second Albigen expected to hear another shot and see one of his friends fall. Realising there was only one thing to do, he pressed the switch on the detonator. There was a flash of light and a huge explosion. Then, the whole compound was plunged into darkness.

A few moments later, Ezekiel and Maeve came stumbling towards him.

'Over here!' Albigen called.

He took out a torch and lit the way towards the sewer, closing the lid behind them when they were safely below ground.

'I know you told me not to set off the charge until I heard from you, but I had to do something,' he told Ezekiel. 'The people in the hospital wing. Were they…?'

'Don't worry about them,' Ezekiel replied. 'They're much better off than they were, believe me. Now come on, let's get out of this dreadful place.'

THE COFFIN

Malachy opened the rear doors of the long black hearse and lifted the lid of the coffin. 'Looks as if it was custom made for you,' he said with a wry smile.

'Thanks very much,' Dante replied.

'All right, listen,' Malachy went on, the smile fading quickly from his lips. 'Kurt will get here in less than ten minutes. So, get in the coffin and I'll screw the lid down, just in case he decides to get curious. But you'll be all right. There's enough air in there to keep you alive until we're clear of this place.'

As the lid was placed in position, Dante lay in complete darkness scarcely able to move, listening to the screws being tightened. He felt a wave of claustrophobia threatening to overwhelm him but he concentrated on breathing as slowly as possible, and gradually he became calmer. 'It's only for a limited time,' he told himself. 'Maybe ten or fifteen minutes.'

Malachy shut the door of the hearse and waited for Kurt to arrive. A few minutes later he appeared, wheeling his bicycle up the path towards the Supervisor's Lodge and whistling tunelessly to himself. Finding Malachy standing on the drive waiting for him, he looked nervously at his watch.

'It's all right, you're not late,' Malachy told him. 'But I've just had a call about a body in the southern outskirts.'

Kurt nodded. 'I'll just put my bicycle away and then I'll go and collect it,' he said.

Malachy shook his head. 'I'm going myself.'

Kurt looked at him in surprise. 'I thought that normally...' he began.

'Don't think, Kurt!' Malachy interrupted. 'It doesn't suit you.'

'Sorry sir,' Kurt said, politely enough, but his eyes betrayed a cold fury.

As soon as he had said it, Malachy realised it was a mistake. Now he had made an enemy of Kurt and he didn't need any more complications at the moment. But as he was considering how to remedy the situation, he became aware of a car coming up the drive towards them. It drew to a halt immediately in front of the hearse and a middle-aged man dressed in the uniform of the security services got out. He opened the passenger door for a large, rather fierce looking dog to clamber out after him.

'Which one of you is Malachy Mazotta?' he demanded.

'I am.'

'Good. My name is Commander Ruggieri. I'm the new security chief for the area.'

'Pleased to meet you.'

Commander Ruggieri raised one eyebrow as if he doubted that anyone was ever *truly* pleased to meet him. 'I've come to inspect the ledger of deaths,' he said.

'Certainly,' Malachy told him. 'I'm afraid I have to collect a body just now, but my assistant, Kurt, will be happy to show them to you.'

Commander Ruggieri shook his head. 'Your assistant will look after my dog,' he said. 'You will show me the ledger yourself.'

Malachy glanced at the coffin in the back of the hearse, then shrugged. 'As you wish.'

Ruggieri turned to Kurt. 'Fetch my dog some fresh water and make sure you keep a careful eye on him. He's a very valuable animal.'

Unaware of all this, Dante lay in the darkness, wondering how much time had passed since the lid had been screwed down. It seemed to him that they ought to be on their way by now and he could feel the tide of panic beginning to rise once more.

He tried to think about it rationally. Malachy had not said exactly how long the air in the coffin would last. Just that there was enough for them to get clear of the Necropolis. But how much time was that? Twenty minutes? Half an hour? He knew that if he breathed too quickly he would use up more oxygen, but it was hard not to. Anxiety made his heart race and the feeling of being closed in and unable to move made him want to scream for someone to release him. He decided to start counting. Slowly and regularly. It would help him stay calm as well as giving him a better idea of how much time had passed.

Meanwhile, in the Supervisor's Lodge, Commander Ruggieri was looking critically around Malachy's study.

He ran a finger over the window sill and held it up for examination. 'This place is filthy,' he declared with a curl of the lip, 'and appallingly untidy. You ought to be ashamed of yourself.'

'I can assure you, I know precisely where everything is,' Malachy told him.

'I should hope so. Now then, when was the ledger last checked?'

'It's never been checked while I've been working here.'

Ruggieri shook his head in disgust. 'Then we have a lot of work ahead of us,' he said. 'Let's get started.'

By the time Dante had reached twelve hundred, a nagging doubt had begun to grow in his mind – Malachy wasn't going to come back. He'd never intended to. The whole thing had merely been a trick to get rid of him.

'What a fool I've been!' he muttered to himself. 'Climbing into my own coffin like a lamb to the slaughter. All Malachy has to do now is to wait for me to suffocate, then bury my body anywhere in this awful place!'

He must have been in the coffin for nearly half an hour now. Pretty soon he would start to lose consciousness completely. 'I have to get out of here before that happens,' he told himself. He uncrossed his hands, placed his palms against the coffin lid and pushed with all his strength. But the lid would not give an inch.

Panic overwhelmed him like a flood. Fear took hold of his body and squeezed the breath out of him. His heart began to pound until he felt as if the walls of his chest must burst at any moment. Every reflex in his body screamed at him to do something about his situation. But what?

Odyllic force! Up until now he had only managed to draw upon it in his waking dreams; but Ezekiel Semiramis had once told him: 'The Odyll finds us first in our dreams but we must learn the way back to it from the everyday world. That is the road to power.'

All very well for Ezekiel to say that. He had mastered odyllic force so effectively that he could stop time itself. It was how he had freed Dante and Bea from the asylum of Tarnagar. 'But how do I even start?' Dante asked himself.

Of course! The grey door that hung in the air by itself. Dante concentrated as hard as he could, trying to build a picture in his mind. Had it been made of wood, or metal, or stone? No, there was something changeable, something fluid about it, as if it was constructed from nothing but energy, an elusive fragment of the Odyll itself.

Perhaps he could start by recalling what it had felt like to stand in front of that door, looking at the symbols that writhed and swarmed all over its surface. He had felt both fear and attraction – fear of the enormous power those symbols suggested, coupled with a desire to wield that power, to bend it to his will. He had been certain that it was his to command if only he could overcome the barrier that made him hesitate. But what was that barrier?

Immediately the answer came to him. It was death. That was what he feared. Only when he was prepared to go through that door and never come back would the power of the Odyll be his. Dante had to accept that his life might come to an end in darkness, silence and nothingness. Was he ready for that? Well, why not? As things were, death would find him very soon, anyway.

First he took a deep breath. Then he began saying goodbye to all the people who had meant something to him – Bea and Ezekiel, Albigen and Maeve and all his other friends among the Púca. Lastly, he relinquished all the pleasures and joys he had known – the satisfaction of a good meal, the thrill of running down a hill, the feel of the wind on his face, the comfort of a soft bed at the end of the day, even the flow of breath in and out of his body. He bid all of it farewell. In its place he focused every part of his attention on summoning the Odyll.

Suddenly the door was there, hanging in his mind, a shape of solid mist, upon whose surface flowed a never-ending sequence of symbols. He held onto that image until it grew stronger, until there was nothing else in the world but the door and himself. Then, feeling it begin to draw him in, he surrendered, letting his mind rise up out of the coffin as the door swung open before him.

Now the world of the Odyll was all around him, without form but teeming with shapes and colours that flickered in and out of existence. Everywhere there was movement, as possibilities blossomed and vanished within an instant. He himself was a part of the great language of the Odyll and felt its power surging through him. He knew that he could stretch from one end of the universe to another, filling the great darkness of space, no longer bound by the limitations of his earthly body.

'My body!'

With this thought, Dante felt the world solidifying around him and he found himself standing beside the hearse outside the Supervisor's Lodge. Just next to the hearse was a large black car and standing beside that car was a man he presumed must be Kurt. He was looking rather nervously at a large dog that was sitting on the ground beside him. Dante felt certain that Kurt could not see him but the dog had risen to its feet and was staring wildly in his direction, emitting a low growl. He turned his back on the animal and gave his attention instead to the coffin.

How to undo the screws? He suspected that in this odyllic body he would not be able to affect or manipulate the physical world. To test this, he put out his hand to touch the hearse. There was absolutely no feeling of contact. His hand moved through the metal as if there were nothing there at all. In this state things could only be achieved by thinking about them.

He stared through the window of the hearse at the lid of the coffin, focusing on the screws that held it in place. He concentrated on one of them in particular and imagined it turning, ascending out of the hole in the wood and falling to the floor. At first nothing happened but then the screw began to move. Just a fraction to begin with, then another fraction, then steadily round and round. As it turned, the screw rose up into the air until it fell with a slight rattle onto the floor of the van.

The second one was easier and he began to realise that it was more a matter of belief than of willpower. He had to create a picture in his mind of the screw coming out of the coffin by itself and then he had to believe that this was the truth. The other version of the world, in which the screw was firmly fixed in place, was the fantasy.

But as Dante's activities grew more obvious, so the dog's growling increased. Its fur was standing up on end and its teeth were bared. Kurt was looking around him in bewilderment, trying to understand the cause of the animal's ferocity. Dante turned back to the hearse and continued to work on the screws until at last there was only one left.

In the effort of concentration, however, he failed to notice Kurt wander over to the hearse and watch with astonishment as the last screw rotated its way out of position and popped neatly out of its hole.

'How can this be happening?' Kurt muttered to himself.

Dante turned and saw Kurt opening his mouth to shout. Instinctively, he reached into the dog's mind and deflected its anger towards Kurt.

Instantly, the dog threw itself at Kurt who struggled desperately to fight it off. Again and again it leapt at him, trying to sink its teeth into his throat. At that moment Commander Ruggieri come running out of the lodge, closely followed by Malachy. The Commander rushed across the drive, grabbed hold of the dog and pulled it away from the terrified Kurt.

'What have you been doing to my dog?' Ruggieri demanded.

'I didn't do anything, sir,' Kurt protested. 'He just suddenly attacked me for no reason.'

'My dog does not attack for no reason!' Commander Ruggieri insisted. 'You must have been tormenting him.'

'But I wasn't!' Kurt protested.

All the time the dog kept barking furiously, struggling to get out of its owner's grip and hurl itself once more upon Kurt.

'Go and get those cuts cleaned up!' Malachy told him.

Kurt needed no further encouragement.

'I shall mention this in my report!' Commander Ruggieri told Malachy.

Malachy looked unimpressed. 'What you say in your report is your concern. However, I must insist that you take that animal away immediately since you're obviously unable to control it.'

The Commander opened his mouth to say something but the dog began struggling even more ferociously as its barking rose to a frenzy. He turned on the dog. 'Shut up, you stupid cur!' he shouted. He dragged the dog over to his car, opened the rear door and shoved it inside.

'I have not finished with you, Mr Mazotta,' he went on. 'Not by any means. I will return very soon, and when I do, you had better make sure that everything is in order.'

'Everything here will be as it always has been,' Malachy assured him. 'I'll look forward to your visit.'

Ruggieri looked as if he was considering saying

something else but then turned, got into the car and drove off at high speed.

Dante had been watching all this and knew that it was time to return to the coffin. He summoned the memory of the body he had left behind. It was weak, the life in it running low, like a candle that is nearly spent. He reminded himself that it belonged to him, that it was natural for him to inhabit it and suddenly there he was, pinned once more within the wooden walls of the coffin.

A moment later the lid was lifted and he opened his eyes to see Malachy's anxious face peering down at him. 'Are you all right?' Malachy demanded.

'Just about,' Dante told him.

'Did Kurt open this lid?'

Dante shook his head. 'I did.'

Malachy looked at him in bewilderment. 'You did?'

'I think we should go now,' Dante urged him.

Malachy nodded. Explanations would have to wait for later. He closed the door, got into the driver's seat and drove off.

THE CHANGELING

Luther sat on a rock beside the stream that ran through the middle of Liminal Park, basking in the midday sun and considering the events of the previous night. 'I must be careful,' he reminded himself. 'Every situation has to be thoroughly assessed.' Nevertheless, he did not think that Nyro represented a serious threat.

Despite his friend's efforts to conceal himself, Luther had spotted him the moment he walked down the road. How ridiculous he had looked, skulking in the doorway like that. Human beings were so clumsy, so unaware of the world around them. Nyro had stood out in the night like a firefly, advertising his presence wherever he went.

For a moment Luther had been tempted to acknowledge his former friend. To have a companion in his lonely vigil would have been a consolation. But a true hunter must shed his past like a snake sheds its skin.

So Luther had turned his back and made his way to the park while Nyro had limped along behind him. And when Luther had entered the park and climbed to the point where the land reached out to embrace the moon, Nyro had not dared to ascend, to feel the moon's current washing over him like cool breeze on a hot summer's day. Too blind, too deaf, too weak and too ignorant, just like all the rest of them, utterly unable to change. His poor mind was nothing but a babble of conflicting voices.

It was just the same with Luther's mother. She never stopped asking him questions. Where was he going? What was he doing? But he said nothing. Silence was the first weapon.

Banishing their insipid faces from his mind, he shut his eyes and spoke to the water instead. Like everything else here, it was full of longing for a world beyond the city, one that was not bound and gagged with brick and concrete, stuck with fences and swarmed over by the aimless exertions of people. The water sang songs of freedom to him. It would not stay here in the park. It would run to the sea. It would fly to the air.

Luther opened his eyes. 'Not yet,' he told himself. 'Soon, but not yet. I must wait for the Call.'

Last night when he had stood upon rising ground and greeted the moon, he had thought that the Call would surely come. He had felt a hush of expectation, both in the world of form and in the formless world that runs beneath it like a mighty river. It seemed to him that all things held their breath and waited. Luther had joined his expectation to theirs, straining every sense for the faintest whisper, certain that his name was about to be spoken. But the Call had not come.

At first he had thought it was because of Nyro waiting below, tainting the atmosphere. But as Luther grew more attuned to the other world and as the power of the moon filled him, he understood that it was not Nyro's presence that stopped him from hearing the Call. It was simply not yet time.

Now he crouched down beside the stream, watching the stones at the edge of the water where the sunlight fell. Patience was all it took.

It was hard to believe that there were tens of thousands of men and women in this city and not one of them was aware of the world of the formless, even though they walked through it every day, even though it swelled and billowed about them.

And he had been just like them. Before his Awakening.

A small, slate-coloured lizard crept out from its hiding place in the bank, drawn by the warmth of the sun on the stones and by the insects that hovered temptingly nearby. The lizard waited, measuring the speed and distance of its prey, letting its stillness reassure them. But Luther also waited, as still as the lizard. His breathing became slower and his concentration deepened until he was on the very edge of the formless world, feeling its energy lapping about his feet. Then his hand shot out and seized the lizard. With one movement he brought it to his mouth, bit off the head and swallowed.

BARZACH

'Barzach is where people are taught to love and obey our leader – unconditionally,' Malachy explained as they drove along. Dante had climbed out of the coffin shortly after they had left the Necropolis. By now he was beginning to relax and forget his taste of imminent suffocation.

'What does that mean?' he asked.

'It's a place of correction, where the minds of trouble-makers are reprogrammed.'

'Like the asylum on Tarnagar?'

'A bit. But Barzach is about more than just confining people. A whole town has grown up around it, dedicated to the cult of Doctor Sigmundus. Have you never heard of the Museum of the Leader?'

'No.'

Malachy shook his head. 'You have led a sheltered life, haven't you? Well the Museum of the Leader is at the heart of Barzach. It's a complex of buildings that houses a vast exhibition devoted to the life and works of Sigmundus. Visitors come from all over the country to see it.'

They heard what sounded like thunder, off in the distance. But instead of dying away, the noise grew steadily louder.

Malachy stopped the car and they both got out. In the sky above them an aeroplane was banking in a wide curve, white smoke streaming from its tail. Dante stared at it in shock. 'I thought all Sigmundus' flying machines had been destroyed,' he said.

'They were,' Malachy replied, frowning. 'He must have rebuilt some. But that machine is nothing like as sophisticated as the ones he used to possess.'

'How do you know?'

'I was a pilot for seven years.'

They watched as the plane gradually dwindled into the distance. When it was no more than a speck, they got back in the car and continued with their journey.

'So if you were a pilot, how did you end up in charge of the Necropolis?' Dante asked.

'A long time ago I was married,' Malachy told him, 'and my wife, like me, was immune to Ichor. But she found it much more difficult to live with her secret and she began to dream of escaping over the border to Tavor. Naturally, I did my best to discourage her.'

'Why?'

'Because no one can cross the border. Soldiers patrol night and day. It would have been suicide even to try.'

'Couldn't you have flown across?'

Malachy grimaced. 'Maybe. I could have tried, I suppose. But the truth is I was too much of a coward. One morning I woke up to find my wife was not in the bed beside me. I searched the house but there was not even a note.'

'Do you know what happened to her?'

'My guess is that she was picked up by the security services before she got anywhere near the border. Whatever happened, it was decided that I was a security risk by association with her. A few days later I was transferred to the Necropolis and I have remained there ever since.'

'I'm sorry,' Dante said.

'So am I.'

Malachy was silent for a long time. Then he said, 'Since we are trading explanations, tell me how you managed to unscrew a coffin from the inside.'

'I don't understand it myself,' Dante told him.

'You did it with your mind?'

'Yes, you could say that.'

Malachy nodded. 'I've heard rumours of such things.'

They had turned off the main road by now and most of the traffic had been left behind. On either side was flat pasture land, dotted here and there with cattle. 'This road will bring us out about a mile from the town itself,' Malachy said. 'Any closer and the hearse might attract too much attention. So you can walk the rest of the way. I'll wait for two hours exactly. After that, I have to return to the Necropolis.'

Dante nodded. 'All right,' he said. 'But there's one more thing I'd like to know.'

'What's that?'

'Why are you doing this?'

Malachy shrugged. 'Perhaps if I help you I might be able look in the mirror once more without despising the man who stares back at me,' he said.

* * *

The town of Barzach had been built for one purpose alone: to glorify the name of Doctor Sigmundus. Dante sat on a bench in the central square watching the hordes of pilgrims eagerly buying souvenirs. There were figurines of Doctor Sigmundus, plates, mugs and trays with his face on them, and leather-bound copies of *The Promises*. At the other end of the square children were queuing up to have their photographs taken standing under a huge statue of the leader himself.

'Where shall I begin?' Dante asked himself. He closed his eyes and tried to think back to the state he had been in when he had conjured up the Odyll in the coffin. But he felt drained by his earlier experience and could not achieve the same level of urgency and concentration. As he opened his eyes again, his gaze fell on the huge bronze doors of the Museum of the Leader. It seemed as good a place to start as any.

He joined the queue and filed in through the entrance. Inside was a huge gallery filled with displays devoted to important moments in Sigmundus' life. In the very centre, inside a glass case, was the prize exhibit – handwritten notes of the speech in which he had announced the end of crime. Visitors were gathered around a tour guide who was busily explaining the history of the speech and the glorious impact it had made upon their society.

Dante wandered through galleries dedicated to the boyhood of Sigmundus, and Sigmundus the politician, into one devoted to the history of Ichor. There were fewer visitors here. Part of this room was roped off and a museum worker was cleaning the floor with a mop and bucket. She wore a long black robe and a headscarf that covered her hair and part of her face. But Dante recognised her immediately. He crossed the room quickly and stood beside the rope barrier, beckoning to her urgently.

She frowned at him but did not move.

'Bea, it's me, Dante!' he said, trying to keep his voice as low as possible. 'Don't you recognise me?'

'I'm sorry sir, I think you must have got me mixed up with somebody else,' she told him, shaking her head. 'If you need information, you should ask at the front desk.'

Dante ran his hands through his hair in exasperation. 'I'm not looking for information,' he told her. 'I came here to find *you*. We were friends back on Tarnagar, remember?'

'Tarnagar?' she repeated slowly.

'Yes, the asylum where your parents were doctors. Then Ezekiel Semiramis arrived. You hid in the Recovery Room. And we escaped to Moiteera, the ruined city. Come on Bea, please, you must remember!'

She stared back at him in confusion.

'Oh Bea!' he said. 'What have they done to you?'

'I am a museum sister,' she told him firmly. 'My only purpose is to serve the Leader. I have never seen you before. And now I must ask you to leave immediately or I shall be forced to summon the security guards.'

Dante stepped across the rope and put his hand on her arm. 'That's not you talking,' he insisted. 'It's what they've taught you to think. Listen, you used to live on Tarnagar. The first time we met was in the woods. You were trying to learn the words of your coming-of-age ceremony and you couldn't get them right. You said, "Who cares about bloody Doctor Sigmundus anyway?".'

He smiled at this memory, but she stared back at him in horror. Then she shook his arm off, rushed across the room to the big red button near the door and set off the alarm.

Dante turned and ran as fast as he could back the way he had come. At first, confused pilgrims and museum workers stared at him but no one tried to stop him. Then he heard shouting and, ahead of him, dozens of security guards came pouring down the staircase into the reception hall.

With no idea now where he was going, Dante skidded to a halt and set off in the opposite direction. A few of the braver museum workers tried to grab him but he shook them off. A gun fired and something hit him in the arm. But somehow, he carried on running towards the back of the building, hoping desperately that there was a rear exit. Pushing his way through a door marked *Private*, he found himself in the kitchens.

At first he thought they were deserted until he noticed an old woman standing by the sink, looking at him intently. Her face was thin and lined but there was a brightness about her eyes, as if they belonged to a much younger woman. In one hand she held a kitchen knife. Dante stopped in his tracks and glanced at the blade. To his surprise the woman put the knife down and placed her finger on her lips. Then she stepped to one side and opened the door of a tall cupboard. 'Quickly,' she told him.

Was it a trap? Why would she want to help him? But his arm was throbbing and his legs were beginning to grow weak. He wouldn't be able to outrun the security guards. He stepped into the cupboard and the woman swiftly closed the door behind him. A moment later he heard shouts and he knew the security guards had caught up.

As he waited tensely in the darkness, he ran his fingers over his wound and found a tiny dart embedded in his skin. Grabbing it between his finger and thumb, he pulled it out, wincing at the pain. Then, too weak to stand any longer, he slumped slowly to the floor.

'What a fool I am!' he told himself. He should have approached Bea gently instead of overwhelming her. But at the sight of her cleaning the floor in a museum dedicated to the adoration of Sigmundus, common sense had fled from his mind. As he recalled her confused and angry face, waves of darkness rolled over him and he released his hold on consciousness.

The next thing he knew someone was shaking him, forcing him back into wakefulness. The old woman with the bright blue eyes stood over him. 'You must get up!' she told him. 'There isn't much time.'

Dante struggled to his feet.

'Good! Now follow me.' She led him out of the kitchen along a series of passages, and through a door at the side of the building. His legs could hardly support him and his head was throbbing.

'Listen carefully,' she told him, as they stood looking out at a paved courtyard. 'In the corner of the yard there is a part of the fence that is broken. You can escape into the field on the other side. But they'll be searching the whole area for you, so take great care!'

'What is your name?' Dante asked.

'Seersha,' she told him.

'Thank you for helping me, Seersha.'

She nodded impatiently. 'You must hurry!'

Dante made his way across the courtyard to the place where the fence was broken. He climbed through into the field on the other side where he lay down on the ground, trying to summon the energy to set off again. The temptation to close his eyes and go back to sleep was almost overwhelming but he forced himself to crawl through the tall grass, trying to remember the direction he needed to go in order to meet up with Malachy. But his thoughts were hazy and it was like struggling to see through fog.

At the end of the field was a barbed wire fence, on the other side of which was a wooded area. He crawled under the wire, tearing his clothes and scratching his legs in the process. But at least now he could stand upright under cover of the trees. I'll go left, he decided, and made his way parallel to the museum building, hoping to reach a service road to the west of the museum that he had noticed on his way in.

Suddenly something hit him on the head and his feet

went from under him. Stunned, he lay on the ground waiting for hands to seize him. After a while he sat up, looked around and realised he had merely hit his head on an overhanging branch. He got to his feet and lurched clumsily on. Soon he saw an end to the trees. Up ahead was the road.

At first glance it seemed completely deserted and he was just congratulating himself on avoiding his pursuers when he saw a trio of security guards walking in his direction. Immediately, he dropped to the ground and crawled into the gully at the side of the road. He lay in the stagnant water as the security guards walked steadily along the road towards him, stopping only about a hundred yards away. He waited, shivering in the bottom of the ditch for what seemed like quarter of an hour, but the security guards did not move. Finally, he decided he would have to crawl along the ditch right underneath their noses.

Slowly, he began to inch his way forward through the slime, trying to ignore the mosquitoes that buzzed hungrily around his face. All at once a pheasant rose out of the ditch, screeching indignantly at being disturbed. On the road above, one of the security guards turned and looked his way.

Frantically, Dante looked round for something he could use as a weapon – a stone, or a piece of wood – but there was nothing in the bottom of the ditch. Desperately he reached out for the power of the Odyll, trying to summon the image of the grey door. His body began to shake with the strain.

Just at that moment came the sound of an engine. The approaching security guard stopped in his tracks as a car rounded the bend and drew up by the side of the road. An officer got out and the security guards stood stiffly to attention.

'What are you doing, standing around here?' the officer demanded angrily. 'What do you think this is – a stroll in the countryside?'

One of the security guards began some sort of explanation but he was immediately cut short.

'Get down to the crossroads and take up your positions!' the officer ordered. 'And you'd better hope the intruder hasn't already got past you.'

The guards set off down the road at a run. The officer stood watching them for a moment, then got back in the car and drove off.

Dante counted to a hundred, then he climbed out of the ditch and staggered on.

Malachy was pacing nervously near the hearse when he saw Dante lurching along the road towards him. He quickly rushed over to meet him.

'What's the matter with you?' he demanded but Dante could only point to his arm and mumble incoherently. With some difficulty Malachy got him into one of the coffins and replaced the lid.

He had not driven very far, however, before he found the road ahead blocked. A security guard signalled for him to halt. For a brief moment Malachy considered driving straight through but then he thought better of it.

'Is there a problem, officer?' he asked, when he had wound down his window.

'Nothing for you to worry about, sir,' the security guard told him. 'Just a routine check. Your name is?'

'Malachy Mazotta.'

'And where are you heading?'

'Back to the Necropolis with a corpse.'

The guard nodded. 'Right then,' he said. 'Sorry to bother you.'

When they had left the roadblock behind, Malachy called out, 'Are you all right back there?'

But there was no answer.

GRACE

'Today I am going to talk to you about grace,' Mother Zhosia announced. Sister Beatrice was standing in the Assembly Hall with the other workers, trying to listen to the mid-afternoon sermon. But she kept thinking about the mysterious young man. Had she really known him in her previous life? In some very deep part of her being, this possibility excited her.

After the stranger had fled, Mother Zhosia had spoken to her at length, asking her to repeat everything she had seen and everything he had said. Beatrice had held back nothing and Mother Zhosia had looked very solemn indeed, shaking her head in dismay when she heard the boy's remarks about Doctor Sigmundus. Afterwards, Mother Zhosia had decreed that Beatrice should undertake extra cleaning duties for the next month. 'When a person comes into contact with dirt, some of that dirt will inevitably stick,' Mother Zhosia had pointed out. 'So you should accept this penance gratefully and look on it as a symbolic cleansing of yourself.' Though this had not seemed entirely fair to Beatrice, she had bitten her lip and said nothing.

Now Mother Zhosia stood at the lectern, a small but imposing figure, the only person in the room dressed all in white. She surveyed them with a sorrowful gaze. 'Grace is the state to which every human being should aspire,' she told them, 'a state in which every action he or she performs is in harmony with the rest of society. That is the goal of our society and the wish of our beloved Leader. That is why he has given us the gift of Ichor.' As she said this she paused and placed her right hand on her chest above her heart, a gesture that was immediately mirrored by every other woman in the room.

'Of course Ichor, by itself, cannot create a perfect world,' she continued. 'Each one of you must assist in the process of making ours a healthy society. Unfortunately, you are all here in this room because at some time or another you have fallen from grace. You reached a turning point and made a wrong decision, a decision which had the direst consequences for you and for others around you.'

She paused here, and now the women bowed their heads in shame. But for the briefest of instants, Sister Beatrice looked up. In that moment she caught the eye of Sister Seersha and it seemed to her that some sort of understanding passed between them.

After sufficient time had elapsed for them to consider their failings, Mother Zhosia resumed. 'Thanks to our beloved Leader you have been given a second chance and in return for that helping hand, it is up to each one of you to live a life that is immaculate. What a beautiful word that is! Im-mac-ulate.

'This morning, as you are all aware, there was a most

regrettable incident which disturbed the surface of our lives. A deranged stranger entered the museum and tried to spread poison in our midst. But we will not let him affect us any further! We will purge the museum of his unwholesome influence! We will begin by reciting the Promises of Doctor Sigmundus.'

Everyone in the room immediately raised their arms in the air at this announcement. As Mother Zhosia had explained to them, holding one's arms aloft was a symbol of surrender and the proper way to stand when reciting the Promises.

Of course it was not easy to keep your arms held up like that for any length of time. And the Promises took a very long time to recite. But the aching in your arms was to be welcomed, Mother Zhosia had insisted, because it reminded you of the sinfulness that had brought you to the museum in the first place.

Mother Zhosia began the recitation and her audience immediately joined in. 'Doctor Sigmundus has promised us that where there was uncertainty, there shall be reassurance, where there was anxiety, there shall be peace, where once we lived in fear of violence, in future we shall fear no more. We will no longer walk down streets where danger lurks in every corner. The deviant and the criminal are banished from our ranks forever.'

As the recitation continued, Beatrice found it increasingly difficult to concentrate. Her arms ached and there was still a corner of her mind that would not stop thinking about the young man. A picture flashed into her mind for the briefest of moments: a landscape of broken but still majestic buildings, a tower projecting from their midst like a finger reaching towards the sky. With this picture came a whole host of emotions, painful, joyful, and bewildering, flooding her senses while she continued to mouth the words of the Promises.

At last the recitation was over and they filed out of the room in order of seniority, with Beatrice bringing up the rear. As always, they made their way across the central courtyard to the Dagabo. Once a week every man, woman and child in Gehenna attended their local Dagabo to receive Ichor but for the museum sisters it was a daily occurrence.

As they filed into the building, the Official Recorder in his purple robes stood waiting for them beside the Dispensing Table. One by one, they sat in their appointed seats and waited to be called to the front in their turn.

Finally, Beatrice's name was called but as she set off walking down the aisle an idea began to take shape in her mind, as if a little voice inside her had spoken. 'Don't swallow the capsule!' it said. Keep it under your tongue. Then afterwards you can take it out when no one is looking. It was the only way to remember more about the boy and about the ruined landscape she had glimpsed so briefly.

But that would be a terrible sin. 'Every time you think of yourself instead of thinking about the good of society, you are turning your back on our Leader,' Mother Zhosia had once told her. 'It is as if you were deliberately rejecting him, as if you wanted to hurt him.'

Tears had come to Beatrice's eyes when she had first

heard this. 'I would never want to hurt our Leader,' she had told Mother Zhosia.

Mother Zhosia had shaken her head gravely. 'Never *again*, Beatrice,' she had pointed out. 'Never *again*. Always remember that you were brought here in the first place because of the wickedness you stored up in your heart. That wickedness will always be there. No matter how hard you try, you cannot get rid of it. Only by the gift of Ichor and by keeping a watch on your thoughts at all times, can you resist the temptation to fall back into your old ways. You will do that for me, won't you, Beatrice? You will stay on the golden path that our Leader has laid down for us?'

'Yes Mother,' Beatrice had promised. And she had meant it with her whole heart.

Now, with bowed head, she stepped up to where a golden star had been painted on the floor, the outward symbol of that golden path. After a moment she raised her eyes and looked at the face of the Official Recorder. His face was lined, grey hairs grew in tufts on his ears and there was a sour smell about him. There was a sour smell about him. He held up the capsule of Ichor for her to see. 'Behold our Leader's gift to you,' he told her.

'I receive it with humility and gratitude,' she replied.

CATACOMBS

Driving as fast as he dared, Malachy turned the hearse off the main road onto a narrow track that descended steeply. The hedges on either side were so overgrown that it was like entering a green tunnel. Even though he drove slowly, the van bounced alarmingly along the rough dirt road while bushes swept its sides like claws. At last the track came to an abrupt halt at the base of a chalky hill. Here was the beginning of a series of tunnels, where the dead had been buried long before the construction of the Necropolis.

Malachy flung open the back doors and lifted the lid of the coffin. Dante still appeared to be completely lifeless. Malachy slapped him sharply across the face but there was no response. Taking hold of Dante's wrist, he felt for a pulse. Nothing. He put his fingers on either side of Dante's windpipe, shut his eyes and concentrated. Was there the faintest of movements? Or was he just imagining it?

Malachy could not afford to waste any more time. The security guard manning the roadblock would certainly have contacted his superiors by now and Ruggieri would be back.

Taking a collapsible trolley from the back of the

hearse, he slid Dante's coffin onto it. Then, with some difficulty he wheeled it over the rough ground towards the entrance to the ancient catacombs. Once inside, he took a flashlight from his pocket and began pushing the trolley slowly forwards along the tunnel. The bitterly cold air smelled stale and musty.

He came to the first gallery of tombs. An opening had been made on one side of the tunnel and rough shelves had been created in the wall. On each of these shelves a sepulchre rested, carved with the ancient language of Gehenna and illustrated with mysterious scenes, several of which showed a winged figure. On previous visits Malachy had tried to decipher these cryptic messages but always without success.

He continued on past the first three galleries. In the fourth, a gap had been left and Malachy carefully slid the coffin from the trolley into the empty space. He left the lid off and stood for a moment looking down at Dante's inert form. He suspected that Dante was truly dead but decided that he would return later to make sure, as soon as he was certain that it was safe.

A few minutes later he drove through the gates of the Necropolis to find Kurt waiting for him. 'You were a long time,' Kurt observed.

Malachy gave him a hard look. 'Since when has it been your place to comment on my movements?' he asked.

'I'm sorry sir,' Kurt said, stiffly. 'Shall I help you deal with the body?'

'There was no body.'

Kurt looked blank. 'What do you mean?'

'It was a hoax. Someone's idea of a joke.'

'Then it ought to be reported,' Kurt declared indignantly. 'Wasting official time is a serious matter.'

Malachy shrugged. 'Yes, of course. But these things happen sometimes, Kurt. You should try not to take them too seriously. Now, if it's all right with you, I think I'll go and have some lunch.'

But Malachy had only just finished making himself a sandwich when he heard a car drive up in front of the house. With a sigh, he got to his feet. Ruggieri had returned.

Dante swam in the depths of a fathomless ocean, surrounded by the voices of the dead. Most complained endlessly that their lives had been snatched away too soon, their ambitions ruined and their hopes dashed. His presence among them was an insult, they added, a bitter reminder of everything that had been taken away from them. Their angry voices rose higher and higher until he awoke with a jolt.

When he opened his eyes he found that he could see and hear absolutely nothing. He had no idea where he was, only that it was very cold and he was once more lying in a coffin. What had happened to him?

He tried to sit up and immediately banged his head. There seemed to be a shelf of rock directly above him. Keeping his head bent, he climbed out of the coffin and fell forwards, landing painfully on a hard stone floor.

Getting to his feet, he found that he could stand upright. Now that his eyes had begun to adjust to his surroundings, he realised that it was not entirely dark. Some distance ahead of him there was a very faint light. Cautiously, he began to walk towards it. The closer he got, the more he was able to discern his surroundings. Gradually, he began to understand that he was in an underground burial site.

To his dismay, when he reached the point where the light was brightest, instead of an exit, he found a vertical shaft that had been cut into the rock. Far down at the bottom of the shaft, a pale blue light glimmered. Crude metal spikes had been hammered into the rock at intervals to provide hand and foot holds. But the shaft was only just wide enough to accommodate one person.

Dante hesitated. He needed to get out of this place, but there was something about the quality of that faint blue glow that beckoned him, as if it was there entirely for his benefit. Taking a deep breath, he stepped gingerly into the shaft, placing his right foot on the first metal spike.

After a long climb downwards, he reached the bottom of the shaft and found himself in a high-ceilinged chamber. In the centre of the chamber was a stone table. Next to this table stood a tall winged figure.

'Welcome, Dante Cazabon,' the winged man said, in a voice that seemed to possess a similar quality to the pale blue light that filled the room. 'Do you believe in me now?'

'You are Tzavinyah,' Dante said, 'the messenger of the Odyll.'

Tzavinyah nodded. 'And I bring you this message: you must make your way to where the Púca are encamped with all speed.'

'What about Bea?' Dante asked. 'I can't just leave her in Barzach.'

'Ezekiel's life is in danger, Dante. He needs your help, now.'

'Of course,' Dante said. 'I'll leave right away.'

'There is one more thing that you should know,' Tzavinyah continued. 'You have a twin brother.'

Dante stared at him in astonishment. Throughout his childhood he had assumed he was alone in the world, with no one to share his joys or sufferings. 'But why didn't my parents tell me this?' he demanded.

'Because they do not know. Your mother was told that one of her children had been born dead. But it was a lie. The child was stolen.'

'Why didn't you let her know the truth?'

'I can only speak to those who are ready to hear me.'

'But surely my mother...' Dante began.

Tzavinyah shook his head. 'Your mother's grief made her deaf and blind to me. Even now, though she dwells deep within the odyllic realm, her pain is a barrier between us.'

'Then *I* will tell her!' Dante exclaimed.

Tzavinyah held up a finger in warning. 'Do not let anything delay your journey. Without your help, Ezekiel is lost.'

With these words the messenger vanished. Though a faint blue radiance remained, it was rapidly dying away and Dante knew that he had to get out of the chamber quickly before it became too dark to find an exit.

Commander Ruggieri decided not to bring his dog on his second visit. But he did bring security guards who searched the Supervisor's Lodge, the garage and sheds where coffins were stored, and every inch of the Necropolis itself. It took hours before they were finished and still Ruggieri was far from satisfied. He made it clear that he did not believe Malachy's story about a hoax call. He would have the telephone records checked, he declared. And if he found that Malachy was lying, the repercussions would be extremely serious.

After he had gone, Malachy dismissed Kurt, got into the hearse and made his way to the catacombs. Dante could have woken hours ago. What would he think, finding himself interred under the ground?

Parking at the end of the track, Malachy hurried inside. When he reached the fourth gallery he shone the light into the empty coffin. Dismayed, he called out and a moment later, to his relief, there came an answering shout.

'Where are you?' Malachy called.

'I don't know,' Dante replied.

'I'm going to keep calling out,' Malachy shouted back. 'Try to follow the sound of my voice.'

He continued to call out encouragement and after a little while Dante appeared, stumbling along the tunnel towards him.

'First you lock me in a coffin, then you stick me in this place,' Dante protested. 'Are you trying to tell me something?'

'I had to put you somewhere,' Malachy replied. 'Ruggieri has been searching every inch of the Necropolis.'

'He can search all he likes. I have to leave here, anyway,' Dante told him.

'Where are you going?'

'Down south, near a town called Vendas. It's where I believe I will find the Púca. My friend's life is in danger and I have to help him.'

'How did you find this out?' Malachy asked.

Dante described his meeting with Tzavinyah. Malachy listened without interrupting but looked sceptical. 'You were shot with a drugged dart,' he pointed out. 'If you ask me, your anxiety about your friend made you imagine a winged man who told you he's in trouble. That's all it is, believe me.'

By now they had reached the entrance and were stepping outside. Dante had just opened his mouth to argue when a sudden movement made him stop. Further up the track a bicycle was disappearing round the bend.

'Kurt!' Malachy hissed. 'He must have been spying on us. Now Ruggieri will be here within the hour! I'm afraid you may never get to Vendas, my friend.'

PUNISHMENT

At five o'clock in the morning Sister Beatrice awoke. She never needed an alarm clock. As soon as the first faint light crept into the sky she was always awake, ready to perform her duties. But as she clambered out of bed this morning, something unusual happened – her eye fell on the carved wooden bird on the top shelf in the alcove opposite the bed. For a moment she felt as if the room was spinning. She put her hands to her head and took deep breaths to steady herself.

The bird was the only thing that remained from her previous life. She had found it at the bottom of the meagre bag of possessions she had brought from the hospital. Perhaps it had simply been overlooked.

Sister Beatrice had always regarded this bird with mixed feelings. It was, of course, a symbol of her shame, reminding her of that other existence in which she had defied the Leader and rejected his teachings. And yet, whenever she picked it up, it evoked a feeling of tenderness that could bring her to the point of tears. She avoided touching it, though she could never quite bring herself to throw it away.

This morning, however, it seemed to draw her attention like a magnet. For the first time since arriving at the museum, it occurred to her that the bird was also a symbol of freedom. She drew up a wooden chair, climbed onto the seat, and took it down from the shelf.

As she stood there holding the simple wooden carving in her hands, the face of the stranger came vividly into her mind. The early morning light that slanted through her window suddenly seemed to be full of promise. The possibility of happiness hummed like a sound far away in the distance, coming closer all the time.

Further along the corridor, she heard the sound of a door closing. Sister Seersha was getting up. As Beatrice put the bird under her pillow, she saw the little capsule of Ichor lying there. She picked it up and held it between her finger and thumb for a moment. Then, crossing quickly to the sink in the corner of the room, she turned on the tap, let go of the capsule and watched as it was flushed away. Afterwards, she washed her face, dressed rapidly and made her way to the kitchen where Sister Seersha was already hard at work.

Of all the museum sisters, Seersha was the least talkative. When the two of them had first worked together Beatrice had found this unnerving. In time, however, she had come to prefer working in silence alongside this serene older woman. Now, as she crossed the Long Dining Room where Seersha was already laying out the breakfast bowls, they smiled at each other. But Beatrice was worried about what she had done.

Why am I like this? she asked herself. Immediately the answer came back: it was the First Fault. Bea had been taught about the First Fault on the day she had arrived at the museum. Mother Zhosia had explained it to her as they sat in her office. There had been no sound but the ticking of the clock on the wall and the rise and fall of Mother Zhosia's voice, stern yet comforting.

'Each one of us is born incomplete,' Mother Zhosia had said. 'Deep in our hearts we know this to be true and as we go through our lives we try to find something that will make us whole. In the past people tried alcohol and various narcotics to overcome the dissatisfaction caused by this incompleteness. They committed acts of vandalism, violence and crime, they gave themselves up to political movements, creating revolutions and tearing down their governments. But no one could ever find a way to rid themselves of the emptiness they felt at their core. Oh, they could forget it for a while, sometimes for quite long periods at a time, but it always came back because it is part of the way human beings have evolved. There is a flaw in our very make-up. It is the First Fault. And there is only one cure for it.'

She put her hand to her breast as she said this and Bea immediately followed suit. Mother Zhosia smiled. 'That is the reason why we place our hands here, above our hearts, whenever we mention Ichor. It is an acknowledgement of the fact that the First Fault lies deep in our hearts and only the gift of our Leader can cure us of it.'

Now Beatrice filled the huge copper porridge pot with water and turned on the stove beneath it. 'I am a very bad person,' she told herself. 'I am in love with the

First Fault. I do not want it to wither and die within me. I want to nourish it, to watch it grew and blossom into wickedness. If Mother Zhosia knew what was in my mind she would turn from me in disgust. And she would be right to do so. I need to be punished.'

She had turned her back on the Leader and every time she did so, she caused him pain. So it was only right that she should suffer too.

First she moved the porridge pot so that the flames beneath it were exposed. For a moment she watched those little blue tongues of fire that remained perfectly still at their hearts, only flickering with purple and yellow light at their very edges. They were beautiful to look at, so constant and true, not like human beings. Then she took a deep breath and thrust her hand into the flame. Despite her resolve, she cried out.

Somebody grabbed her and pulled her away from the stove. 'What are you doing?' Sister Seersha demanded. She was standing behind Beatrice, her eyes filled with shock and concern.

The pain was so great that Beatrice could not speak.

'Put it under the cold tap, quickly,' Seersha told her. She led Beatrice to the sink and turned on the tap.

Beatrice put her hand under the stream of cold water. The relief was enormous. Now, for the first time, tears began running down her face.

'You did that on purpose, didn't you?' Seersha asked.

'I deserved it,' Beatrice told her.

Seersha looked at her in bewilderment. 'What are you talking about?'

Perhaps it was the pain that made her lose her sense of caution or perhaps it was just that she needed to talk to someone so desperately. Whatever the reason, Beatrice confessed what she had done to Seersha. 'You won't tell anyone, will you?' she pleaded.

'Of course not.'

'It's the First Fault,' Beatrice went on. 'It's so strong in me. I try to fight it but it keeps coming back.'

Seersha looked at her for a long time without speaking. Finally she said, 'Have you ever thought that the First Fault might be the real you?'

'What do you mean?'

'Just what I say. Maybe that's why you can't get rid of it. Because it's who you really are.'

Beatrice stared back at her in dismay. 'You think I'm really that wicked?'

Seersha shook her head. 'That's not what I'm saying, Beatrice,' she said. 'Listen, before I came to the museum...'

But before she could say any more Sister Melicum came into the kitchen. She stopped and stared at them. 'What's going on?' she asked.

'Sister Beatrice has burned her hand,' Seersha explained.

Sister Melicum tutted. 'You're so careless, Beatrice,' she declared. 'I hope this doesn't mean that breakfast is going to be late.'

'Of course not,' Beatrice told her. She turned off the tap, dabbed her hand with a towel, bit her lip, and went back to the task of making porridge. 'I am glad of the pain,' she told herself. 'It will be a lesson to me, never to turn my back on our Leader again.' But even as she was telling herself this, she couldn't help but wonder what it was that Sister Seersha had been about to tell her.

THE FLYING MACHINE

'You have to leave now,' Malachy insisted.

'What about you?'

'I'm too old to start running away. I'll just go back to the lodge and wait for them to turn up.'

'You'll be in terrible trouble for sheltering me.'

Malachy sighed. 'It had to happen sooner or later,' he said. 'Maybe I can think of a story that will satisfy them.

'That's not very likely,' Dante began but Malachy interrupted him.

'Ssh!' he said. 'Listen!'

In the distance the sound of an aeroplane engine could clearly be heard. It was faint at first, but getting louder all the time. Dante searched the sky but it was Malachy who pointed it out, behind them, flying lower than when they had spotted it previously.

'There's something wrong with that machine,' Malachy said. 'I can tell from the sound of the engine.'

Instead of a consistent drone, the aeroplane's engine seemed to splutter, stop, and start again.

'You think it's going to crash?'

'Sounds like it.'

The aeroplane banked in a steep curve flying away

from them, then gradually returning until it was facing them once more.

'He's looking for somewhere to land,' Malachy declared.

'But there isn't anywhere,' Dante pointed out. 'The countryside round here is littered with rocks.'

'There's the road leading up to the Necropolis,' Malachy said. 'It's long and straight and it was built in the days when funerals were grand occasions so it might be wide enough. The only problem is the trees on either side. It could be suicide if he doesn't get his approach right.'

The plane had banked above them once more and was now descending very deliberately towards the Necropolis.

A wild plan began to form in Dante's mind. 'Let's go and meet him,' he said. Malachy looked at him as if he was crazy.

'I need you to trust me,' Dante told him.

Malachy shrugged. 'Get in then,' he said. They jumped in the hearse and Malachy drove back in the direction of the Necropolis, parking at the junction with the main road. The plane was only just above the level of the trees now and bearing down towards the road.

Dante's hands were balled into fists and his stomach muscles grew tight with the tension. He could actually make out the shape of the pilot in the cockpit and he wondered what must be going through the man's mind as he struggled to keep his aeroplane under control.

The plane descended between the lines of trees as

neatly as a thread through a needle. For a brief period it flew just above the level of the road, then, with a shriek, the wheels touched the road, releasing a cloud of dust and the smell of burning rubber. As if in protest, the plane seemed to bounce upwards. Then down it came again, its wheels gripping the road.

Further along, however, the road turned sharply westwards. The plane still travelled at breakneck speed, eating up the distance between itself and the bend. But at last it began to slow down, finally coming to a halt just before the turn. Dante let out a long sigh of relief.

'That was some piece of flying!' Malachy said. 'I'll go first and see what sort of shape the pilot's in.'

Up close, this aeroplane was nothing like the streamlined metal bird that had stood proudly on display in the museum of Moiteera. For one thing it had two sets of wings, one above the other. For another, it seemed to be constructed as much from canvas and wood as from metal. Malachy stared at it, shaking his head in disbelief. 'Where the hell did they dig this up from?' he muttered. 'It's positively ancient.'

The pilot sat motionless in the cockpit, staring in front of him. 'Why doesn't he get out?' Dante wondered.

'C'mon over, Dante.' Malachy called. 'I think the pilot's dead.'

'What happened to him?' Dante asked as he approached the plane.

'Broke his neck, by the looks of it. Must have been the whiplash.'

Dante felt a wave of pity for the young man who had

brought his plane down with such skill, only to be cheated like this at the last minute. But his pity was rapidly displaced by excitement at his plan. 'We could use this plane,' he said.

'What do you mean?'

'We could use it to escape from the security forces and we could go and find Púca.'

'Dante, why do you think the pilot brought the plane down here?' Malachy said. 'The engine isn't firing properly.'

'I know, but couldn't you fix it?'

'I was a pilot, not a mechanic.'

'But you *do* know something about how the engine works.'

'Of course I do. You can't fly them without having some idea of the basics. But it might need spare parts and the whole idea is...ridiculous.'

'But not impossible?'

'Well, no. I mean, it's not a very complicated machine. But even supposing I could get it up and running, we'd need to find somewhere to land once we reach our destination. Have you even thought about that?'

'When we were on the way to Barzach you said you wanted to be able to face yourself in the mirror again,' Dante reminded him. 'Have you given up on that already?'

Malachy stared at him for a long time in silence. Then, reluctantly, he nodded his head. 'All right,' he said. 'You win! I'll see what I can do.'

'Thank you!'

'Never mind the thanks,' Malachy told him. 'Just help me get the pilot out of the cockpit.'

The pilot was young – no more that twenty-five. Beneath his helmet and goggles, he had blond hair, very fair skin and his eyes were as blue as the sky. Together, they dragged him out of the cockpit and put him in the hearse. Then Malachy set to work.

He worked systematically, first familiarising himself with the engine, then testing the individual components. Occasionally, he muttered and swore to himself but mostly he was silent. Dante sat by the side of the road and watched. As the sky gradually grew darker, Malachy made him hold a flashlight so he could continue working. After about half an hour, he nodded and turned to Dante. 'Looks like the distributor blocks on the magnetos are all fouled up.'

'Can you fix them?'

'They just need cleaning.'

'Is that all?'

Malachy raised one eyebrow. 'Don't try and pretend you know anything about it,' he said.

It took a long time but at last Malachy seemed satisfied. 'Now for the moment of truth,' he said. He switched on the engine. It came to life with a reassuring purr.

'Well done!' Dante said.

Malachy grinned. 'Get on board.'

Dante climbed into the rear cockpit.

'Strap yourself in!'

It was hard to hear much above the noise and they were forced to yell at each other.

'We can't turn around,' Malachy shouted. 'There isn't room. We've got to take her round the bend and use the straight on the other side.'

For the first time, Dante detected real enthusiasm in the old man's voice.

The plane began to taxi gently around the bend until they faced a long straight stretch of road, though in the distance it curved once more.

'Here we go!' Malachy exclaimed.

The sound of the engine grew steadily louder and the wind rushed in Dante's face alarmingly as they began racing along the road at terrifying speed. He heard Malachy let out a string of curses. 'What's the matter?' he shouted.

'Look up ahead!' Malachy called back.

Dante craned his neck to one side and screwed up his eyes. A car had come round the bend and was driving rapidly in their direction, getting closer with alarming speed. The driver caught sight of them and screeched to a halt but it was too late to stop the plane. If they could not get airborne in time, there would be a collision.

There was nothing Malachy could do but grit his teeth and hope for the best as the plane continued to race along the road. Up ahead, the passengers had scrambled out of their vehicle. Most of them were security guards.

At the last minute, just as it seemed as if they must surely crash into the vehicle, Dante felt his stomach lurch as the nose of the plane began to rise in the air, almost skimming the top of the car. For a moment Dante could clearly see the bewildered expressions on the faces of the onlookers. Among them was Kurt, his mouth wide open. Then they were heading up towards the clouds and it came to Dante that for the first time in his life he had left the earth behind and was free as a bird.

IN THE LIBRARY

The punishment that Sister Beatrice had ordained for herself was having an odd effect. Instead of turning her mind back towards the Leader, she found herself listening more and more often to the voice of the First Fault. Whether she was cleaning the steps of the museum, washing the plates after a meal, or even reciting the Promises, the First Fault made itself heard. 'Why should you have to slave like this?' it demanded.

A few days after she burnt her hand, she had just finished clearing up in the kitchen after the evening meal when she heard a faint tapping sound. A moth was flying round and round the light, beating its wings repeatedly against the shade as it tried to get closer to the source of its fatal attraction. As she watched, the moth's dance became increasingly frantic until finally it collided with the light bulb and flew off at an angle.

Beatrice went to look at the moth, which had come to rest on the counter next to the sink. It was a plain enough specimen with its dusty brown wings spread out on either side. But it struck her that it was beautiful in its own way. While she stood there watching it, Sister Melicum came into the kitchen.

That morning Sister Melicum had been promoted to

Kitchen Superintendent. Already she was revelling in her new found importance, continually finding jobs that had not been done correctly. 'Still here, Sister Beatrice?' she asked. 'You really are very slow, aren't you?'

'The food had stuck to the bottom of the pans,' Beatrice explained. 'It was difficult to get them clean.'

Sister Melicum shook her head. 'Always making excuses. What were you looking at when I came in?'

'Just a moth.'

Sister Melicum came and stood beside Beatrice. She was a big woman and beside her, Beatrice often felt like a little girl. There was always a strong smell of sweat about Sister Melicum and this evening it was worse than usual.

Sister Melicum considered the moth for a moment. Then she reached out and squashed it with her thumb. 'Better wipe that up,' she said. Then she looked down at the floor. 'And the tiles need washing again,' she added.

'Yes, Sister Melicum.'

Putting aside the little flare of anger she felt at the death of the moth, Bea filled a bucket with water and set to work. Sister Melicum watched for a while then strode away. As Beatrice continued to scrub the floor mechanically, a picture began to form in her mind of the entrance to the hotel in Moiteera where she had hidden after her escape from the island of Tarnagar. The image was so vivid that it took her breath away and she stood leaning on the mop with her eyes closed. This sort of thing seemed to be happening to her more and more often. It was as if the pain she had experienced had woken a part of her mind that had been slumbering and, without Ichor to put it back to sleep, the memories of her past had begun rising insistently to the surface.

Faces were floating before her eyes. She saw Ezekiel Semiramis with his hawk-like expression and she recalled how frightened she had once been of him. And yet he had possessed a kind of deep gentleness. She saw red-haired Maeve who was always so kind but could fight like a tiger if the need arose, brave Albigen whom everyone looked up to, and pale-faced Eugenius who had lost his soul trying to come awake in his dreams. And then she saw Dante.

Suddenly, Beatrice felt a sob forming in her chest. She remembered it all now. They really *had* been friends on the island of Tarnagar. They had defied Doctor Sigmundus and escaped to join the Púca. And she had turned him away! Betrayed him to the authorities!

She finished mopping the kitchen floor and looked at the clock on the wall. In fifteen minutes she was supposed to join the others in the Assembly Hall for the evening recitation. She ought to go back to her room to wash and change her clothes. Instead, she left the kitchen, walked quickly along the corridor and up the stairs that led to the museum library.

The library was never open to the public. The museum workers only went in there to clean and dust. Inside, a number of large glass fronted bookcases were filled with unread books about the life of Doctor Sigmundus and commentaries on his speeches. But Beatrice remembered that when she was first shown around the museum, she had noticed a map of Gehenna on the wall at one end of the library. Moving quickly and quietly, she crossed the room and stood in front of it. It was drawn to a fairly large scale and there wasn't a lot of detail.

Ellison was about three quarters of the way up on the left hand side, and there just to the south of it was the museum. Her eyes travelled down the map, past towns and cities she had only vaguely heard of, to the southern coast. There it was – the island of Tarnagar. Moiteera ought to be somewhere above it. But it wasn't marked. The city had simply been erased!

Beatrice was trying to work out exactly where it ought to be when she heard voices. Someone was entering the library! She stayed perfectly still, concealed for the time being by a bookcase. A moment later she recognised the gentle but authoritative tone of Mother Zhosia.

'The museum sisters are always knocking on the door of my office,' Mother Zhosia was saying. 'I sometimes think this whole place would come to a standstill without me. But no one will disturb us in here.'

Nervously, Beatrice peeped around the corner of the bookcase and saw that Mother Zhosia was accompanied by a tall, thin man dressed in black. The two of them sat down at a table in the middle of the room.

'So,' Mother Zhosia continued, 'to what do we owe the honour of a personal visit from the Deputy Director of the Leader's Office?'

Though Mother Zhosia spoke politely, Beatrice thought she could detect a distinct wariness in her voice.

'I have been sent with instructions concerning one of your sisters,' the stranger began, speaking quietly but in the voice of someone who was used to being listened to. 'I have come in person because Doctor Sigmundus wants you to understand the importance of this matter.'

'You have my undivided attention,' Mother Zhosia told him, clasping her hands in front of her and fixing her large grey eyes on the visitor.

'Good. Please understand there is no room for error in this matter. Now, the sister in question is Beatrice Argenti.'

Beatrice bit her lip and listened intently.

'In the past, she has had associations with the boy who caused the disturbance you reported. He is an extremely dangerous criminal,' the Deputy Director went on, 'who represents a significant threat to the stability of our society. Doctor Sigmundus was very disappointed to learn that he was not successfully apprehended.'

'That is something I deeply regret,' Mother Zhosia replied humbly. 'However, the security staff involved have all been properly disciplined.'

'I'm glad to hear it. Nevertheless, you will provide me with the names of those responsible before I leave.'

'Certainly.'

'Now, with respect to the girl – Doctor Sigmundus has decided that she will be brought to Ellison tomorrow afternoon. A military escort will arrive for her at five o'clock. Naturally, she is to be told nothing of this.'

'I understand.'

'Good. Then I will waste no more of your time.'

The two of them rose and left the library together.

Beatrice stood, stunned by what she had just heard. At last, she collected herself and ran back downstairs. Then she changed her clothes as quickly as she could and made her way to the Assembly Hall.

THE HOUSE OF FEARS

For the last ten minutes the plane had bucked and rocked alarmingly, making Dante's stomach lurch so much that he felt certain he would be sick at any moment. It did not help to think that all that was between him and an almighty drop to the earth below was a fragile construction of canvas, wood and metal. He didn't even understand how the machine stayed up in the sky.

'Why does it fly?' he asked, shouting to make himself heard above the noise of the engine.

'Thrust and lift,' Malachy shouted back.

'What does that mean?'

'Didn't they teach you anything at school?'

Dante was about to reply that he hadn't been to school, but before he could open his mouth the plane entered another area of turbulence. He leaned over the side and was heartily sick.

'It'll freeze before it hits the ground,' Malachy called out cheerily. 'Like a miniature hail storm. Hard luck on anyone below.'

Before long the sky ahead of them began to get colder and darker and it was obvious they were flying into a gathering storm. Soon they were being lashed with rain, and all around them lightning flashed alarmingly.

'I'm going to try and fly above it,' Malachy called out, pulling back hard on the throttle and forcing the plane to climb higher. But it was no good. The roof of the storm was higher than they could reach.

'We can't keep on like this,' Malachy announced. 'It'll tear the plane to pieces. We'll have to land somewhere and sit it out.'

'Wherever we land in Gehenna, the authorities will arrive soon afterwards!' Dante objected. Ezekiel's life was in danger and there was no time to waste. But it seemed that they had no other choice.

'Looks like we're going to fly over the border into Tavor, then,' Malachy called, turning the plane westwards. 'Pity I didn't do this thirty years ago!' he said to himself.

Soon the weather began to improve. Below them, they could see the dark shapes of the Forgill Mountains that marked the border between the two countries.

'I'm going to head for that gap between those two peaks, right ahead,' Malachy shouted. 'Once we're on the other side we'll have to start looking around for that nice flat place to land you promised me.'

Dante discovered that distances were deceptive in the air. If you kept looking at the same point on the ground, it could seem like you weren't really travelling at all, just hanging in the air like a bird riding the wind. But the steady throb of the engine told a different story and little by little the two peaks that Malachy had pointed out began to come closer until at last they were flying directly between them.

'The people who lived here thousands of years ago called these mountains the Forgill Aya. Want to know what it means?' Malachy called out. 'The Devil's Fence.'

The name meant nothing to Dante. 'Who, or what, was the devil?' he asked.

Malachy was silent for a while and Dante began to wonder whether he'd heard the question. But finally he said, 'It's hard to explain but I should think our friend Doctor Sigmundus fits the bill pretty well.'

Now they could see the land on the other side of the mountains. It fell away in a series of peaks and troughs and Dante began to realise the absurdity of his earlier optimism about landing. But suddenly he spotted a bright flash of colour. 'What's that?' he called out.

'I don't know,' Malachy yelled back. 'Let's take a closer look.'

They came down further and now they could see that it was a field, though the bright purple crop was not one that Dante recognised. He didn't spend long wondering about it, however, for right beside it he glimpsed a grey scar in the landscape that could only be a stretch of tarmac. He pointed it out to Malachy, who nodded eagerly.

They descended rapidly and it became clear that they had somehow managed to find a regular airstrip. A moment later, with a dreadful judder, the wheels touched the ground and they rushed headlong towards the end of the runway.

As the aeroplane began to lose speed, Dante let out a long breath. His neck wasn't broken and he could hardly believe his luck. When they had finally come to a halt, he climbed out of the cockpit and stood on shaky legs beside Malachy.

'Even if I say so myself, that wasn't bad for someone who hasn't flown for twenty years,' Malachy said.

Dante began to congratulate him when he saw a convoy of military vehicles driving towards them.

'Here comes our welcoming committee,' Malachy said.

The convoy pulled up beside them and half a dozen soldiers jumped out waving guns in their direction. 'Hands up!' they yelled.

A red-faced officer walked briskly over to them. 'What the hell is going on here?' he demanded. 'There was no delivery scheduled for today.'

'We're refugees from Gehenna, seeking sanctuary,' Malachy declared.

'Then you're under arrest for unauthorised infringement of Tavorian air space, trespass on a secure establishment and spying for a foreign power,' the officer replied. 'Take them away,' he told the soldiers.

Malachy continued to argue furiously. But Dante was no longer listening. He allowed himself to be led away without protest, for something very strange was happening. Everywhere he looked, a grey mist was gathering. It was drifting around the feet of the soldiers; it was blowing past the red-faced officer; its tendrils were snaking around the wheels of the plane. But no one could see it except Dante. This place was more deeply connected to the Odyll than anywhere he had ever been. On the surface it appeared to be some sort of military base but beneath that thin veneer of reality was something very much older and altogether more dangerous.

He and Malachy were put in a cell together. As soon as the door was shut, Malachy turned to him. 'Did you hear what that officer said?' he asked.

Dante shook his head. He could barely take in what Malachy was saying. The mist rose from the floor and began to fill the room.

'He said there was no delivery scheduled for today,' Malachy continued. 'It sounds to me as though there's some sort of arrangement between Tavor and Gehenna going on here. They're in it together! Which means they're either going to send us straight back home or execute us as spies. Dante, are you listening to me?'

'Odyllic power is everywhere in this place,' Dante told him. 'I don't know why.'

Malachy shook his head. 'Look Dante, a lot of what you say doesn't make any sense to me but if you really do have some kind of power, then now would be a very good time to prove it.'

Dante nodded. 'Right. But don't worry if I seem to lose consciousness.' Then he stopped trying to resist the Odyll's power. Immediately, the grey door hung in the air beside him. Without hesitating, he left his body behind, opened the door and stepped through.

On the other side of the doorway was the study where he had previously seen his parents but this time the place had been ransacked. Books had been torn from the shelves and hurled across the floor, the furniture was broken and the curtains ripped. In a corner of the room a youth of about his own age was lying on the floor, his face covered with blood. Dante crossed the room and bent down to study him more closely. Suddenly the youth opened his eyes and burst out laughing. 'Fooled you!' he said, getting to his feet and wiping the blood from his face.

'Looking for someone, were you?' he continued, clambering onto the table and sitting down cross-legged.

'My mother and father, actually,' Dante told him.

'Well you won't find them here,' the youth replied. 'This place has been abandoned. It's just a memory now. They must have moved on, deeper into their own deaths.'

'Who are you?' Dante demanded.

'You can call me Set.'

Suddenly an idea occurred to Dante 'Are you my brother?' he asked.

'I might be,' Set replied.

Despite the uncertainty of the reply, Dante felt a surge of hope. 'Can you take me to my parents?' he asked.

'Follow me and see,' Set told him. He got down from the table, opened a door on the other side of the room that Dante had not noticed before and immediately disappeared. When Dante stepped through the door a moment later there was no sign of Set, just a dimly-lit wood-panelled corridor stretching into the distance.

'Where are you?' Dante called. He stepped forwards

and immediately the door to the study slammed shut behind him. When he turned and tried to open it again, he found it was locked. The sound of laughter came from somewhere further along the corridor. 'Is that you?' he called out.

The laughter was repeated and this time Dante was certain it was Set. He saw a door open at the far end of the corridor. Set stepped out, looked in his direction briefly, then entered another room, directly opposite.

'Wait for me!' Dante called. He ran up to where he had spotted Set but there were several doors leading off the corridor at this point and he could not be certain which of these Set had entered. He chose one at random and opened it. The room within had obviously not been used for a long time. All the furniture was shrouded in white sheets. Set was kneeling in the middle of the floor with his back to the door. In front of him was a body, and in his hand he clutched a large meat cleaver. He turned round and, to Dante's horror, he had the face and snout of an animal. With a yell, Dante fled back out into the corridor, but not before he had recognised the body lying on the floor. It was his own.

He could hear Set's footsteps not far behind him. At the end of the corridor was another door. Dante pushed it open, then stopped in his tracks. He was looking into a huge dining room. At a long table a crowd of half-animal, half-human creatures were sitting down to a meal and in their midst was Set, even though he had been chasing Dante only a moment earlier. 'You're just in time for dinner,' he announced. Then he lifted the lid of the covered dish and Dante saw his own head on the plate.

He was aware of someone screaming. It might have been him but he could no longer tell. He turned and ran once more. And now the corridor changed to a great marble staircase. He took the steps two at a time and before long he found himself on another floor, almost identical to the one he had just left. Innumerable doors opened off a corridor that extended endlessly in both directions.

He glanced towards the foot of the stairs – the creatures he had glimpsed in the dining room were clambering up after him. Frantically, he opened a door to his right and found himself in a bedroom, dominated by a great four-poster bed. Against one wall was a wardrobe. Dante opened the door and hid inside, amongst a lot of heavy old coats and furs.

A few seconds later the door of the room opened. Peering through a crack, he saw one of the half-human creatures step inside. It was as tall as a man with the head of a giant bird. 'No one's in here,' it said in a raucous voice. Then it slammed the door and Dante heard the crowd of creatures thunder along the corridor. He felt a huge sense of relief, but then suddenly he stiffened. Surely he could hear the sound of someone else's breathing in the wardrobe beside him?

'Surprise!' whispered a voice.

Dante yelled and burst out of the wardrobe, hotly

pursued by Set, waving the meat cleaver above his head.

He saw another, smaller set of stairs leading upwards. They went round in a spiral, coming out in a narrow attic room at the very top of the house. There was a bolt on the door and, gratefully, Dante drew it across. But in doing so, he realised he had trapped himself.

It was not long before the door began shuddering under the weight of blows as the creatures tried to force it open. Desperately, Dante looked around for some way out. He tried the window and it opened easily enough. There was a narrow ledge running around the outside but it was difficult to see whether there was any way down.

Cautiously, he climbed out and stood on the ledge. There was something very familiar about the view from up here. The house seemed to be even larger than he had realised. Two great wings extended on either side and beyond them were lawns, gardens and outbuildings. Further away was a large number of mean-looking buildings clustered together and then woods stretching into the distance.

Tarnagar! He was standing at the top of the Great Tower of the Asylum on Tarnagar. Directly below him were the cobblestones onto which his mother had fallen to her death when he was only a baby. But how could this be possible?

The door of the attic burst open. Through the window he saw Set advancing, brandishing the meat cleaver. Behind him the others were grunting and snorting with delight. Now Set had reached the window and was beginning to climb outside. Dante took a step backwards, and fell through the air.

A SHORTAGE OF RICE

Beatrice awoke before dawn the next morning, dressed as noiselessly as she could, then crept into the kitchen and began putting food and drink in a rucksack. She did not take too much, so that her absence would not be noticed immediately. But she could not travel on an empty stomach. When she had stowed away all that she dared, she turned – and froze. Standing in the shadows, watching with an unreadable look on her face, was Sister Seersha.

'What are you doing down here?' Beatrice demanded.

'I had trouble sleeping,' Seersha replied. 'And you?'

Beatrice quickly made up a story about waking and feeling hungry but Sister Seersha shook her head. 'You were running away, weren't you?' she said.

'Of course not,' Beatrice replied.

'Ah, but I think you were, Sister Beatrice. You're dressed for outdoors, you've packed enough food into that bag for a couple of meals. You were going to find that young man.'

Beatrice could only stare back at her in silence.

'I can keep a secret,' Seersha assured her.

'And why would you do that?' Beatrice asked, warily.

'Maybe I have secrets of my own.'

'Such as?'

Seersha hesitated. Then she held out her hand in an expansive gesture. 'None of this – the museum, the things we do here, the Promises themselves – none of it means anything to me. My life here is an empty husk.' She lowered her voice to a whisper. 'I live only in my dreams. And it seems to me from watching you for the last few days, that you are beginning to rediscover yours.'

Beatrice's eyes widened. 'You're right,' she agreed.

'So you really *are* planning to run away?'

'Yes.'

'Where will you go?'

'I'm going to the city of Moiteera where I lived before they brought me here,' Beatrice told her. 'I'm going to rejoin the Púca, the last people left in our country who live in freedom.'

'Dear Beatrice, don't you realise that they'll find you before you've gone more than a few miles?'

'Yes, but I have to try.' She told Seersha about the conversation she had overheard the previous evening. 'I can't just stay here and wait for them to take me away.'

'Then let me come with you.'

Beatrice looked sceptical. 'Why would two people be any more difficult to catch than one?'

'Because I can drive,' Seersha told her. 'And at ten o'clock the truck will arrive with the week's supplies, just like it always does. When the driver gets out to unload, we'll get in and drive away.'

Beatrice looked at her in astonishment. 'If it's as easy

as that, how come you've never tried to escape before?' she demanded.

'Where could I go?' Seersha asked. 'I wouldn't know where to find my husband any more. He might even be dead, for all I know. But you know how to find the Púca. So we've each got something that the other one needs. Is it a deal, Beatrice?'

They stood in silence, looking into each other's eyes. Then a smile spread over Beatrice's face. 'The name's Bea,' she said. 'And yes, it's a deal.'

The museum workers had very little contact with the outside world. Apart from the tour guides and security staff, none of whom actually lived on the premises, the only two workers who ever left the museum were Mother Zhosia and her colleague from the men's quarters.

Essential supplies were delivered once a week in a truck driven by a paunchy middle-aged man called Odem who always seemed to be in a bad mood. The crates were unpacked by the brothers and sisters under his watchful eye, each item checked carefully against a list first.

When he drove the van the short distance across the courtyard from the men's kitchen that morning, Bea and Seersha were already standing outside in the delivery area.

'How are you today, Odem?' Seersha asked brightly.

'Terrible,' Odem told her, clipboard and pen clutched firmly in his hand. He opened the back of the truck and pointed with his thumb to the contents. 'I had to pack this lot by myself this morning. I should have help of course, what with my bad back, but the loaders were all sent to the wrong warehouse. I'm still expected to set out on time, of course. No good telling them that it's too much for one man. They're far too busy to listen to the likes of me.'

Seersha nodded sympathetically while Bea climbed into the back of the van. 'Would you like a cup of tea while you're waiting?' Seersha asked.

Strictly speaking, the sisters were not supposed to fraternise with external workers. Conversations were to be restricted to museum business which in this case meant agreeing that the supplies delivered matched the order list, bringing any deficiencies to the driver's attention, and signing the necessary paperwork. Nevertheless, Odem willingly accepted the offer of tea.

'I don't suppose you've got any cake to go with it?'

'I'm afraid not.'

'A cup of tea's not much good without a piece of cake. Still, if that's all you've got. I'll have three sugars and plenty of milk.'

'Coming up.' Seersha disappeared into the kitchen and came back a few moments later with a mug of tea which she put on the window ledge beside him. He accepted it with a grunt.

'It's not an easy job, you know,' he said, as he watched Bea carrying a sack of rice out of the truck and ticked off the item on his list. 'No one appreciates what's involved.'

'I don't suppose they do,' Seersha agreed.

'Is this all the rice you've brought us?' Bea demanded.

'Course not,' Odem told her. 'There are six more of those sacks in the truck. I put them in myself.'

'Well, you must have delivered them to the men's kitchen,' Bea said.

'They're in the back of the truck,' Odem insisted. 'You just haven't looked properly.'

Bea shook her head. 'I've checked twice. There's no more rice in there.'

Odem sighed. 'See what I mean?' he said, turning to Seersha, but she had disappeared. 'It's always the same,' he grumbled. 'No one seems to know what they're doing, except for me.'

He took a long drink of his tea then climbed into the back of the truck and began rummaging around. 'For goodness sake!' he began. 'There's a whole crate...'

But the rest of his sentence was abruptly cut off as Bea slammed the rear doors. Then she ran round to the front and jumped into the cab alongside Seersha, ignoring the banging noises that were coming from the back of the truck. Seersha turned the key in the ignition and the engine sprang into life. There was a horrible crunching noise as she struggled with the gear stick.

'I thought you said you could drive this!' Bea said anxiously.

'It's been a long time!' Seersha told her. But suddenly the truck lurched forwards. She turned to Bea and grinned. 'We're on our way!' she said as the van nosed its way across the courtyard, out through the gates, and onto the open road.

Part Two
THE ANSWER

EDEN PARK

West of Moiteera, just north of the town of Vendas, a little river wound its way lazily between two hills. At one time, the slopes of the valley had been covered with vines, lovingly tended by their owners. Now it had all grown wild.

A dirt road entered the valley from the east and beside this road was a faded sign welcoming visitors to Eden Park Holiday Village. The owner of the holiday village had had the misfortune to set up in business shortly before the local population had been forcibly moved north to work on the Ichor mines. Consequently, Eden Park had been a financial disaster, and now there was nothing left but a group of abandoned cottages.

Inside one of these, Ezekiel Semiramis was seated at a table, staring directly in front of him. Albigen stood by the door and watched him in silence, a look of anxiety written across his face.

Eventually, Ezekiel let out a long sigh, stretched one arm and winced in pain. Then he gave Albigen a weak smile. 'Thank you for keeping watch.'

'Did you find any trace of Dante?'

'The Odyll is like a great sea,' Ezekiel replied. 'Whenever something causes a disturbance in one part of it, the ripples spread out across the surface for anyone who has the ability to detect them. When I entered the odyllic realm just now, everything was different from my last visit. I cannot begin to understand all that I encountered, but Dante is still free. That much was obvious.'

A smile lit up Albigen's face. 'That's wonderful news.'

Ezekiel nodded. 'You can stop blaming yourself for his capture now.'

'But you don't seem as pleased as you should be,' Albigen continued. 'What else did you discover? What about our enemy?'

'He knows that I am alive and still in contact with the Odyll but he cannot locate us.'

'Then things are better than we had dared to hope.'

Ezekiel shook his head. 'I don't know. There is something happening that is hidden from me. This morning when I entered the Odyll, it was partly to seek news of Dante but partly also because I felt something drawing me there. It seemed for a moment as if I was being called upon to fulfil some great purpose. But then I realised that the call was not intended for me. Someone else was being summoned.'

'Who?'

'I'm not sure but I think that something very old is being conjured back into existence in an entirely new form, something that has its roots in the Nakara.'

'Well, whatever it is, we can deal with it,' Albigen said.

Ezekiel looked less confident. 'I hope so,' he said. 'Could you possibly bring me some water? I'm feeling a bit weak.'

'Of course.'

As Albigen ran over to one of the huts, a frown creased his forehead. It seemed to him that Ezekiel had been growing steadily weaker for weeks now. He filled a mug with water from a jug and ran back quickly. Ezekiel thanked him and drank eagerly.

'Did you learn anything about Bea?' Albigen asked.

'Nothing.'

As Ezekiel spoke, there was a knock on the door and when Albigen opened it, a huge bear of a man with curly hair and a dense black beard was standing there. This was Manachee, Maeve's father. 'I'm sorry to disturb you, Ezekiel,' he said, 'but Eugenius has gone missing.'

'When did you notice he was gone?'

'About an hour and a half ago. We wanted to search everywhere thoroughly before bothering you.'

'He will have gone looking for his mother,' Albigen said. 'We've explained to him a hundred times that she was killed when we were forced to leave Moiteera but he can't seem to understand.'

Ezekiel nodded. The evacuation of Moiteera had not been an easy matter. As soon as Dante and Albigen had left Moiteera to take Bea to the hospital, the rest of the Púca had fled the city in a convoy of vehicles. But a stray sniper had fired on them as they reached the outskirts of the city and by bad luck his bullet had found Perdita, Eugenius' mother. After that, the Púca had shared the responsibility of looking after him.

'What shall we do?' Albigen asked. 'We can't just let him wander off and perish somewhere in the forest. If he gets caught, he might lead them back here.'

In the past Ezekiel would have quickly decided what ought to be done but now he seemed uncertain. At last Albigen made up his own mind. 'I'll go after him,' he said.

'Thank you,' Ezekiel replied. 'But take great care. Forces are being set in motion, but as yet the rules of the game are hidden from me.'

THE MOUNTAIN PASS

Luther sat on the floor of what had once been his bedroom. Nowadays, he needed to feel solid ground beneath him at night, so he only slept in the garden, where he could stretch himself out upon the breathing earth, listening to the sounds of the insects and night creatures.

Nyro paced about the room. Words poured out of him but made no impact on Luther. Knowledge of language had not left him, but it was much less important than it had once been. His road and Nyro's had diverged at the Field of Flowers and since that day they had lost any true connection.

Stubbornly, Nyro kept trying to reach him, drawing upon the friendship they had once shared. But for Luther, it was like listening to the voice of the wind as it played over a field of grass. He watched his old friend's lips stretch themselves into different shapes, noting the way the sounds changed, now full of urgency, now soft and appealing but the words tumbled past him, their little packets of meaning unopened.

A fly buzzed past, its front wings beating two hundred times per second, its hind wings constantly adjusting the pattern of its flight as it circled between the two boys. Luther noted, with admiration, the way it changed direction in the blink of an eye. But it was over-confident, believing nothing that walked on two legs could present any real threat. Suddenly Luther's hand snaked out and he caught the fly in his fist. He put it in his mouth and swallowed.

Nyro stopped pacing and stared at him. 'Oh my God!' he said. 'Did you just eat that fly? Did you?'

Luther smiled and nodded his head.

'You're really sick, Luther,' Nyro went on. 'You need help. You have to see a doctor or a psychiatrist or something. This is worse than I thought. Normal people don't eat flies!'

'All things return unto food,' Luther remarked, speaking slowly and gravely, 'for food is the eldest of beings.'

It was the only thing he had said since Nyro's arrival.

'What are you talking about?' Nyro demanded.

Luther refused to repeat himself.

'How long have you been eating flies?' Nyro demanded.

But now Luther had become aware of a sound on the very edge of his senses, one that demanded his immediate attention.

'You'll give yourself a disease,' Nyro went on. 'For God's sake, Luther, listen to me!'

But someone was speaking to Luther from that place he had sensed when he had stood upon the hill and greeted the moon, from the world of the formless. It was only a whisper but it was so much more real than anything he had ever heard before. He had to find the owner of that voice. He sprang to his feet.

'Where are you going?' Nyro demanded. 'Wait! I'm your friend, Luther. You have to trust me. Just tell me what's going on.'

But Luther had already left the room and was striding purposefully down the stairs. Joyfully, he stepped out of the front door, knowing in his heart that his destiny had finally arrived. This was the moment his whole life had been leading up to.

He loped through the streets of Tohu, heading for the edge of the city. Dusk set in, and then night, but Luther felt no need for rest, moving through the darkness, as invisible as a shadow, as silent as the stars.

By dawn he had reached the edge of habitation and the fringes of the wilderness. It was from here that he had set out only a matter of weeks ago to explore a territory he did not understand. But now his purpose was clear. He had been summoned and he would answer the call.

Day turned to night once again and he continued on his way. Food was all around him. He had only to stretch out his hand and pluck it. From time to time he came across little groups of soldiers patrolling the wilderness but he always spotted them long before they might have seen him.

The land around him rose higher and higher until he was breathing the thin air of the mountain range that separated Tavor from the forbidden land of Gehenna. At this altitude it was bitterly cold but Luther rejoiced in his ability to bear it. He understood his true nature and that understanding increased his strength.

At last he reached the other side of the mountains and began to descend into the wooded valleys of Gehenna. Soon, he felt milder air around him and now the voice of the summons was so loud that he stopped and waited, content in the knowledge that he had reached his destination.

After some time an old man appeared in the distance walking towards him. This was the one. The old man's body was weak and he could not walk without the aid of a stick. But power radiated from him like light from the sun. As the old man drew near, Luther threw himself on the ground.

'You may arise,' the old man told him.

Luther got to his feet.

'I have a great deal of work for you,' the old man continued. 'But first I will give you a new name. Henceforth you will be called Gallowglass, the first of a new order of creation.'

Gallowglass accepted his name with pride.

The old man stretched out his hand. In it he held a string of glass beads. 'They belong to a girl whom you will track down,' the old man told him.

Gallowglass took the beads and held them to his nose. The scent of the girl still lingered on them.

'She will be easy enough to find,' the old man continued, 'for she is without skill or power. But she must be taken alive. That is essential. She is the bait in my trap and I will not have her harmed. At least not before she has outlived her usefulness. You will

find her, follow her, and listen for my instructions. Is
that clear?'

Gallowglass nodded.

'Then let the hunt begin.'

A CHANGE OF CLOTHES

'Who would have thought he had so much energy?'
Seersha said. They had been on the road for almost an
hour now and Odem was still intermittently banging on
the inside of the truck.

'He certainly never showed it when the deliveries
needed unpacking,' Bea observed.

'I think it's time we unloaded him,' Seersha said.

At the next turning, a tiny road that looked like it
seldom saw traffic, they pulled over to the side. Seersha
started to get out but Bea stopped her. 'I'll do it,' she
said. She had a determined look on her face, and
clutched a knife she had taken from the kitchen.

Seersha looked shocked. 'You wouldn't use that,
would you?' she asked.

'I was trained to fight,' Bea told her. 'I don't know
how much of it I remember, but if I had to use it, I think
I could.'

Now that they had stopped, Odem was redoubling
his efforts to attract attention, banging on the side of
the truck and yelling furiously. When he heard Bea,
however, he fell silent. She swung the door open and
stepped back smartly, holding the knife out in front of
her. Odem stood in the back of the truck, looking angry

and confused. 'Where are we?' he demanded, eyeing the knife warily.

Bea shrugged. 'A long way from anywhere.'

'You'll get into very big trouble for this.'

'Let me worry about that,' Bea said. 'Just get down.'

Odem jumped to the ground.

'Lie face down on the ground with your hands out in front of you.'

Odem hesitated, then he began to walk towards her.

Bea made a wild swipe with the knife and he stopped in alarm. 'I said lie on the ground,' she repeated.

Reluctantly, Odem did as he was told.

'Don't move until we're gone,' she ordered. Without taking her eyes off him for a moment, she closed the door of the truck and made her way back to the cabin. Then they drove off leaving him spread-eagled on the ground.

It was more than five hours before they stopped again. By now they were not far from Moiteera but they were almost out of fuel.

'We need to get rid of this van, anyway,' Seersha said. 'They'll be looking everywhere for it. Let's stop in the next field and inspect the cargo properly.'

They were in luck. As well as food, there was quite a range of clothing in the back of the van, including a number of security guards' uniforms. It wasn't hard to find two that fitted them.

'I think we'll be able to barter this food for some alternative transport,' Seersha said, when they had donned the uniforms. 'There's more here than most people could eat in six months.'

'But surely people will be suspicious?' Bea pointed out. 'They'll want to know where it came from.'

Seersha smiled. 'We're members of the security services,' she replied. 'We ask the questions, remember. Now, come on, let's find the local population.'

'How long do you think we've got before they discover the truck?' Bea asked, as they set off up the road together.

'Maybe longer than you think,' Seersha told her. 'What you have to understand about Gehenna is that it's not like the world you grew up in. Tarnagar is a very small community. I imagine that everybody there knows everybody else and everything works properly.'

'Well, the heating system in the Asylum was always breaking down,' Bea replied, 'but you're right about it being a small community. You couldn't scratch yourself without somebody noticing.'

'Well Gehenna is different. It's like a palace ruled by a selfish child who cares nothing for the lives of his servants, just so long as they keep cooking his meals and bringing him all the toys he wants. Everything goes to rack and ruin except those things that he cares about. So in some respects our society is enormously technologically advanced. But in other ways it's totally backward. Much of the industrial part of the country is given over to the mining and processing of Ichor. Elsewhere, people scratch a living from the land like their ancestors did hundreds of years ago. And they're the people we're going to be dealing with – old-fashioned peasants.'

They rounded a bend and saw a solitary farmhouse just off the road. 'Let's see what this place has to offer, shall we?' Seersha said, opening the gate and setting off up the path. Bea followed tentatively, much less confident in her new identity.

They hadn't gone very far before two huge dogs appeared and began racing towards them, barking furiously. A moment later an elderly man dressed in a dirty brown smock and broad-brimmed hat came out of the farmhouse and shouted at the dogs, who immediately turned and ran back towards him. Then he stood in the doorway and waited while Bea and Seersha carried on up the path towards him.

'Sorry about that, ma'am,' he said, addressing Seersha, 'only we don't get many visitors round here.' He spoke with a very strong accent and Bea couldn't help noticing that he had only one tooth in the very centre of his mouth, sticking out of an expanse of bright pink gum.

'That's all right,' Seersha told him.

'You'd best come inside.'

He led them into a dark, low-ceilinged room that reminded Bea of a cave. Even though it was a warm day outside, a fire was burning in a huge old grate and steam was issuing from a blackened kettle that hung directly over the flames.

'I suppose you want to see our Dagabo stamps?' the old man went on. 'Only I'm not sure where my son keeps them. But they're up to date, I can promise you that. Not one of us has ever missed a week without going to the Dagabo to receive Ichor. I'm eighty-four but I'm still able to get about, thanks to our Leader.'

'We haven't come about the Dagabo stamps,' Seersha told him.

The old man frowned. 'So what have you come about?'

'We're passing through your area on very important business,' Seersha explained. 'I'm not at liberty to disclose the exact nature of our errand but I can tell you that it's something of the utmost importance to our Leader himself.' She paused for effect and the old man looked suitably impressed. 'Unfortunately, our truck has broken down just up the road and we need to find some alternative way of continuing our journey.'

'Well, I'd like to help you, of course,' the old man said, 'especially as it's important to our Leader. But the fact is, I don't see what I can do. We don't have any machinery here, see. Everything is done by hand. You could try old Goran Jankovich on the next farm, I suppose. He's got a tractor all right but I don't think it's working just now. He can't get the parts, see.'

'We have a very great deal of food and other supplies in the truck,' Seersha went on.

The old man's eyes lit up. 'What sort of food and supplies?' he asked.

'More than you've seen in a long time,' Seersha told him. 'Why don't you come and have a look for yourself?'

Half an hour later Bea and Seersha set off from the farm on a rickety wooden cart, pulled by an old nag called Ludmilla whom the old man had assured them was the best workhorse he'd ever had.

It wasn't Bea's idea of a bargain. 'I could run more quickly,' she complained. 'At this rate we should arrive in Moiteera some time next year.'

'Speed isn't everything,' Seersha pointed out. She was studying a map they had taken from the cabin of the truck, while Bea held onto the reins and did her best to keep Ludmilla from eating the grass at the side of the road.

For the rest of the day they continued to make their way steadily through tiny, winding lanes, alongside yellow fields of corn and green fields of beet, until night fell and it grew too dark to carry on. They stopped beside an old stone house that had obviously been uninhabited for years. One of the walls had fallen in and a tree was growing up through what remained of the roof. They led Ludmilla round the back of the building where the cart could not be seen from the road, then tethered her to a tree. They ate some of the food they had taken from the truck, then lay down on blankets beside the cart in a silence broken only by the sound of the horse's jaws steadily chomping grass, and waited for sleep to come.

As she lay there, Bea thought about Dante and how brave he had been to come to the museum and try to talk to her. If only she hadn't panicked and set off the alarm! Now they were both being hunted. Had he managed to avoid capture?

Into her mind came the image of him lying on the Shock Table in the Asylum, his head shaved, a leather gag between his teeth. That, too, had come about

131

because of her. Twice now she had betrayed her closest friend.

Suddenly she saw a shooting star streaking across the lower part of the sky. Wasn't there an old belief that you could wish on a star like that? Closing her eyes she concentrated as hard as she could. 'Let Dante still be free,' she said to herself. 'Please let him still be free.'

The only thing she had brought with her from her room in the museum was the little wooden bird that Dante had carved for her. She could clearly recall the morning he had given it to her. It had been the day after her birthday and she had opened the door of her room in Moiteera to find him standing there holding it out, a belated birthday present. Now she took the bird from her pocket and pressed it gently to her lips. 'Good night Dante,' she whispered, 'wherever you are.'

THE GREY BROTHERHOOD

They brought Gallowglass there in one of those metal boxes that run on wheels. The smells and the sounds it made were harsh and unnatural, a reminder of the place he had left behind that clung to his body, making him feel sick. But he had allowed them to take him because that was what the Master had wished.

The soldiers spoke little, sitting opposite him the whole time with their hands on their weapons, jumping every time he moved, afraid because they could not understand what kind of creature he was. When he ate, they drew back in disgust. But their reactions were of no consequence to him. They walked about with their eyes and ears closed to the life all around them, like fish that swim forever round a pond, believing they are travelling the ocean depths.

When they finally reached the end of their journey they made signs for him to get out. They seemed to think he could not understand a word of their language. None of them dared to lay a hand on him, even to direct his steps. Thankful to be in the open air once more, he followed them into a field of rough grass where another, larger vehicle stood. He saw right away that this was where the hunt was to start.

Though the soldiers were anxious to leave him as soon as possible so that they could go back to their ordinary lives, their curiosity about him was intense. They stood and stared as he got down on his hands and knees and made his way around the field, sniffing the ground, drinking the air, finding the scent. The field was full of it. There were two of them – two females, one much older than the other – neither possessing any skill in covering their tracks. They had stumbled about the field like newly born animals, dragging things back and forth clumsily. Finally, they had set off along the road. He could smell their footsteps, feel the warmth their bodies left behind, even see the traces of their auras still lingering in the air, faded now but clear enough to him.

Gallowglass rose to his feet, confident of his ability to find his quarry. The soldiers got back into their vehicle and left. Good! Now he could turn back to the business in hand.

The two females had travelled along the road to a house where more of their kind lived. He looked at the house and considered whether its inhabitants posed a threat to him but he was quickly able to answer that question. There had been only one older male present at the time and they had spoken with him, coming to an arrangement that was mutually profitable. They had left the house in a cart pulled by a horse. He could still feel the animal's resentment in every step it had taken. It was moving slowly, cumbersomely, out of protest. So they would not be far ahead. He could catch them up with ease. He smiled and let his body relax. There was time.

He needed to find a high place, somewhere that commanded a good view. The brotherhood would not acknowledge his authority if he came crawling through the undergrowth. He must stand stiff-legged and tall when he called upon them. Above all, the place must be open to the influence of the moon. For the moon would be at her strongest tonight, flooding the earth with silver, drawing secret currents in the blood.

He spent the rest of the day fruitlessly looking for the perfect place before he realised what a fool he had been, behaving like one of the soldiers who had brought him here! Make yourself quiet, he told himself. Enter the deep place within you where the formless world awaits.

He sat on the earth and allowed his mind to sink into waking sleep. The Master was there. Gallowglass could feel the power of his attention but it was not the Master he sought. Not yet. He let his mind grow utterly still until it separated from his essence and left his body altogether. Now he could be everywhere and nowhere in the beat of a dragonfly's wing.

Immediately, he found the perfect spot – a great flat boulder on a rise of land, surrounded by coarse grass. The earth had made this place for just such an encounter and without a doubt the brotherhood would come here when he called. They were not far away. He could feel their presence. He returned to his body and awoke. Now he could find some food and rest until dark.

When the moon rose, he got up from the hollow in the heather where he lay, stretched, and made his way back to the boulder. He stood, allowing himself to bathe in the moon's radiance until he felt ready. Then he threw back his head and howled, a sound that came from the very deepest part of his being and issued from his mouth with all the force of his loneliness. It was an invitation that did not go unheeded. From far off came an answering cry, then another, and another. Gallowglass laughed aloud. The brotherhood had accepted his challenge. Soon they would be here.

While the moon travelled across the sky, he stood without moving, patient as a stone, watchful as the stars, ready as a cat poised to spring. And at last the brotherhood began to draw near.

The pack leader was perhaps ten years old. His coat was grey with black markings and there were old scars at his throat. He came as close as he dared and held his stance in the moonlight, his mouth hanging open to show his powerful jaws. A single leap would have been enough to bring those jaws into contact with Gallowglass' throat but the wolf paused, waiting to see what Gallowglass would do, while on either side of him the others crept forwards, inch by inch.

Gallowglass did not move a muscle.

Now the oldest wolf took a step into the neutral space between the two of them, snarling. Still Gallowglass waited. The wolf took another step forwards, his snarl growing louder as his confidence increased. Gallowglass let his body loosen slightly, thrust forward his neck and widened his nostrils. The wolf accepted the challenge and leapt towards his opponent.

But just before the wolf made contact, Gallowglass stepped neatly to one side and brought his hand up under the animal's body, flipping him over in the air. The wolf landed on his back on the other side of the rock. Surprised and furious, he righted himself and leapt back, but once again Gallowglass side-stepped easily, chopping the creature's throat with his hand. The wolf sprawled on the ground, struggling to breathe. Gallowglass waited. This time the wolf did not get up. Instead, it began to whimper.

Certain of his dominance, Gallowglass went over to where it lay and stood looking down. The wolf began licking his feet. Gallowglass allowed it to do so. Then, satisfied that there would be no more challengers, he set of running across the grass and behind him, like a sleek, grey tide, came the rest of the pack.

AMID THE ASHES

The closer Bea and Seersha got to Moiteera, the fewer people they saw. Those they did encounter looked at them curiously, puzzled by the sight of two security officers riding on a horse and cart. But no one asked any questions. Respect for authority was too engrained in Gehennan society for that. People merely tipped their hats and wished them good day. After a while they stopped coming across fellow-travellers altogether. 'This part of the country has been officially forgotten,' Seersha told Bea. 'No one talks about it; no one goes near it. It's as if the landscape itself was in disgrace.'

Though the road they travelled had clearly been built to take a wide stream of traffic, its surface was now cracked and pitted; grass and small trees grew up through the stones. The horse had come to accept her fate by now and trotted along at a decent pace. By midday they began to reach the outskirts of Moiteera and immediately Bea realised that something had changed.

The city she remembered had been deserted and dilapidated, its glory faded and its treasures ransacked, but it had not been ravaged by fire. Yet everywhere she looked there were charred and blackened buildings. The closer they got to the city centre, the more the devastation increased and the more certain Bea became that the Púca were no longer here. She felt overwhelmed with frustration – to have come so far with such high hopes, only to find nothing but dust and ashes.

The hotel where they had all lived had been so badly damaged that part of it had collapsed entirely. Bea got out of the cart and began searching through the rubble but Seersha pulled her back.

'It's too dangerous,' she said. 'Besides, what could you possibly hope to find?'

'Something to show that they were here,' Bea said. 'Something to prove that I didn't make it all up.'

'Of course you didn't make it up,' Seersha told her. She put her hands on Bea's shoulders. 'Look at me!' she said.

Reluctantly, Bea looked up.

'We are not going to give up! Do you understand?'

Bea nodded, hesitantly.

'We will find the Púca, wherever they are.'

They got back in the cart and drove determinedly through the streets of Moiteera in the hope that some part of the city would have been left unscathed, but everywhere they looked it was the same. Finally, they returned to the Tower of State, the only building that seemed relatively untouched by the fire. And there they saw Eugenius.

He was sitting on the cracked flagstones at the base of the tower, as still as a statue, his pale face utterly expressionless. Bea jumped down from the cart and ran across to him.

'Eugenius!' she called, 'It's me, Bea.'

His eyes flickered briefly in her direction but otherwise he did not acknowledge her existence.

'What happened, Eugenius? Where did the rest of the Púca go? Where's your mother?'

But her questions were to no avail. It was too much for Bea. Frustrated and infuriated by his silence, she slapped him hard across the face. Immediately, she was overcome with guilt at what she had done. 'I'm so sorry Eugenius, I shouldn't have done that,' she said. She took his hands in hers. They were as cold as marble. 'Please forgive me.'

Seersha came up behind her and lifted her to her feet. 'What's the matter with him?' she asked. 'Why doesn't he answer?'

'Because he can't,' a voice said.

They both spun round. The young man standing behind them had light brown skin, tight curly hair and a jagged scar that ran across his forehead. Bea's face broke into a smile of joy and she ran forward to fling her arms around him. 'Albigen!'

Albigen stepped back to avoid her embrace and put out a hand to halt her. 'First you'd better tell me who this is,' he demanded, pointing towards Seersha, 'and what you're both doing in the uniform of the Security Services.'

Bea restrained her enthusiasm. 'You haven't changed, Albigen,' she said. 'Still as cautious as ever.'

'Caution is what's kept me alive,' he said.

'Fair enough. This is my friend Seersha. These uniforms are our disguise.'

'Did anyone else come with you?'

'No.'

'Okay.' He stepped forwards and put his arms out. The two of them hugged each other. Then he shook hands with Seersha. Throughout this exchange, Eugenius remained in his place at the base of the Tower without registering the slightest interest in the scene.

'So what's happened to the rest of the Púca?' Bea asked. Suddenly a terrible thought seized her. 'They are still alive, aren't they?'

'All except for Perdita, Eugenius's mother. She was shot when we were leaving.'

All three of them turned to Eugenius when Albigen said this. There seemed to be a flicker of life in his eyes.

'Your mother isn't here, Eugenius,' Albigen said gently. 'She was killed when we all left. One of the soldiers shot her. I'm sorry it happened but now you need to come back with me.'

He put out his hand and to everyone's surprise Eugenius took it and got to his feet.

'Best not to stay here any longer than we have to,' Albigen told Bea and Seersha. 'We can leave your horse in a field on the outskirts of the city. Then I'll take you to our new base. On the way, Bea, you can tell me everything that happened to you after we left you in the hospital.'

They went on their way, swapping stories, unaware that from the shadows of a broken building on the other side of the street Gallowglass was watching their every move. The Master was delighted at the arrival of the boy with the scar on his forehead. Gallowglass felt that pleasure, like a current of warmth filling his whole being.

Should he move against them now?

Not yet, the Master told him.

Very well. Gallowglass would wait. He could catch up with them easily enough whenever he needed to. He was tireless and without the weakness of mercy, either for himself or anyone else.

The boy with the scar on his forehead led them away in a van. They moved with speed and clamour, throwing up clouds of dust for the whole world to see. After they were gone there was silence except for the call of birds and the millions of tiny insect voices.

INHERITANCE

While plummeting towards the cobblestones at the base of the Asylum tower, Dante wondered briefly whether the impact would kill him. Just as he was thinking this, he heard a familiar voice saying, 'Take hold of the rope.' A rope of golden thread dangled beside him. He put out his hand – and seized it.

There was no jolt, no strain on the muscles of his arm. Instead he hung there easily, looking upwards, trying to see where the rope was coming from, but the end seemed to disappear into the clouds.

'Climb up the rope,' the voice ordered and now Dante realised that it was Tzavinyah who was guiding him.

Dante had never climbed a rope before and he struggled at first, but eventually he worked out how to lock his feet into position beneath him before reaching upwards to haul himself higher. He was so intent on this that he didn't notice how the world around him had changed. When he was able to take in his surroundings once again, he found himself climbing head-first through the seemingly solid tiled floor of a kitchen – with only a slight feeling of resistance, as if he were lifting his head out of a tub of water.

Tzavinyah was standing in the centre of the kitchen

beside a wooden table. 'The answer to your question is yes,' he said as Dante emerged completely into the room.

The floor seemed to have solidified now so that he could stand securely. He released his hold on the golden rope. 'The answer to which question?' he asked.

'Whether or not you would have died if you had hit the cobblestones.'

'Then thank you for saving me.'

'You may yet be lost,' Tzavinyah told him. 'That depends entirely upon you.'

'What do I have to do?'

'Look around you. Is any of this familiar to you?'

It was a very simple kitchen, much smaller than the one in which Dante had worked on Tarnagar. Just a stove, a sink and a big wooden cupboard. But on the floor was a cane basket. Nestled inside it was a sleeping baby.

He shook his head. 'I don't recognise anything but somehow it makes me feel terribly sad.'

Tzavinyah nodded. 'This is your mother's kitchen. That is your infant self lying in the basket.'

'How long before she returns?'

'Your mother will never return to this room,' Tzavinyah told him. 'In a little while the child in the basket will wake to see soldiers standing over him.'

'Is there nothing we can do about it?' Dante asked.

'What has already happened cannot be altered.'

'Then why have you brought me here?'

'Because this is where your past and your future meet. In this room you must decide whether to take possession of your inheritance.'

'What does that mean?'

'Up until now, whenever you have used the power of the Odyll you have been like a child who finds some money in the street and rushes off to the nearest sweet shop. You have neither understood where your power came from nor how to control it. It is now time for you to become the person you were born to be.'

'Maybe I don't have the strength to do that.'

'The strength will be given to you,' Tzavinyah told him. 'But first you must make a sacrifice.'

'What sort of sacrifice?'

Tzavinyah picked up a pair of golden scissors that were lying on the table. 'You must cut a piece of the golden thread,' Tzavinyah said.

'Is that all?'

'It is more significant than you realise,' Tzavinyah told him. 'Go to the cupboard beside the sink and look for something that you recognise.'

Dante opened the cupboard but as far as he could tell, there was nothing inside except some well used, and slightly chipped, crockery: plates, cups, saucers... Then he noticed a blue bowl sitting on a shelf by itself – the same one his father had used to show him the image of his younger self standing in the woods.

'Fill it with water and bring it here,' Tzavinyah ordered.

Dante did as he was told.

'Now look into the bowl and tell me what you see.'

At first Dante could see nothing except a blurred reflection of himself. But as he continued to look, the reflection changed and an old man's sad and weary face stared out at him.

'This is who you will become if you cut the thread of your life. Not immediately, of course. There will be many years of strength and power but sooner than if your life took its natural course, weakness will find you. You will become old before your time. That is what is happening to your friend Ezekiel Semiramis even now.'

'And what if I decide not to make this sacrifice?' Dante asked, looking up.

'Then the power of the Odyll will desert you and you will fail in your task.'

'Can't I just be ordinary, like everyone else?'

Tzavinyah shook his head. 'No, Dante. You can only choose to accept your destiny or to refuse it. You cannot become someone else.'

Dante put down the bowl and took the scissors from Tzavinyah. 'How much do I cut?'

'The length of your arm will suffice.'

The rope was thick and strong, but the scissors sheared through it easily. To Dante's surprise he felt the cut in his body, exactly as if he had taken a knife and sliced through his own flesh and when he looked at the cut he had made in the rope he saw that blood was coming from it.

'Now make a second cut,' Tzavinyah told him.

Dante hesitated, knowing now how much it would hurt. But he took a deep breath, measured an arm's length of the rope and made the second cut. He wanted to scream in pain but he bit his lip and remained silent.

The piece of cut rope fell to the ground, shrivelled up and disappeared within seconds, leaving the remaining two sections floating in the air.

'Well done!' Tzavinyah said. He took hold of the two cut ends and pressed them together. There was a flash of light, the ends fused together, and a moment later the rope was whole once more.

'Now it is time for you to return to Tavor,' Tzavinyah said.

'Will you answer one more question before I go?' Dante asked.

'If I can.'

'Set isn't my brother, is he?'

'No. He is *my* brother.'

Dante looked at him in amazement. '*Your* brother?'

'Once he was a messenger like me but he considered himself above such work. Now he dwells in the depths of the Nakara and feeds upon the hopes and fears of others.'

'What is the Nakara?' Dante asked.

'It is the place where evil and cruelty are born and, if our enemy has his way, it will swallow up your world entirely. Are you ready to stop him?'

Dante nodded.

Tzavinyah stretched out his hands and the kitchen in which Dante was standing melted away.

Brigadier Giddings banged a gavel on the table in front of him. 'I hereby call this tribunal to order,' he declared. On one side of him sat an elderly man with a shiny, bald head and a huge collection of medals pinned to his uniform. On the other side was a middle-aged woman in a tweed suit who kept frowning at Malachy over the rim of her glasses.

A few minutes earlier, a young soldier who introduced himself as Captain Ramirez had come to the cell, explained that there would be a military tribunal to decide their case, and told them to follow him. Malachy had pointed to Dante, slumped unconscious on the floor, but the Captain had simply sent for a stretcher and Dante had been carried to the courtroom where he now lay on a bench beside Malachy, scarcely breathing.

Brigadier Giddings read the charges against them.

'How do you plead?' he demanded.

'This is ridiculous!' Malachy said. 'My friend isn't even conscious. He should be receiving medical attention, not facing a military tribunal. And I've already explained that we are fleeing persecution by a tyrannical government and wish to apply for sanctuary in Tavor as refugees.'

Brigadier Giddings looked unmoved. 'We'll take that as a plea of not guilty,' he announced. 'Captain Kowalski, you will outline the case for the prosecution.'

A bull necked officer stood up and described how their plane had been observed flying low over the area in a manner which suggested it was conducting aerial reconnaissance. He read out a report stating that no official clearance to fly over Tavorian air-space had been given and that the plane's approach to the airstrip had represented a serious hazard to lives and property. Finally, he pointed out that the defendants did not deny being citizens of a foreign power. 'In the light of what you have heard,' he concluded. 'I suggest that this tribunal find the prisoners guilty as charged. And I would remind the court that the penalty for espionage is death by firing squad.'

Now it was the turn of the defence. But Captain Ramirez stumbled and stuttered, losing his place several times, to the obvious irritation of the judges.

'Thank you Captain,' the Brigadier said when Ramirez had finally finished. He turned to the elderly man with the medals who was sitting beside him.

'Guilty, of course,' the man declared.

The woman in the tweed suit took a little longer to think about it but then she nodded her head vigorously. 'Guilty,' she agreed.

Brigadier Giddings cleared his throat. 'It is the decision of this tribunal that the prisoners be taken from this place and executed by firing squad and that the sentence should be carried out immediately, without recourse to appeal. Guards, take them outside and summon the firing squad!'

Malachy was led outside to a concrete yard and made to stand against a wall with his hands secured to hooks above his head. Dante was carried out beside him and tied to a chair. His head slumped forwards against his chest as a group of six soldiers with rifles formed a line opposite them.

Brigadier Giddings walked over to Malachy and produced a white scarf from his pocket. 'Do you wish to be blindfolded?' he asked.

Malachy shook his head.

'As you please.' The Brigadier turned to the soldiers. 'Firing party, raise your weapons!'

Dante opened his eyes and saw six rifles trained on him. He knew he had only a few seconds in which to act. But he also knew that those few seconds could last as long as he wanted them to – between the eternity of the Odyll, and the procession of minutes which people called Time, there was a middle position, an unending now.

Exerting his will, Dante detached himself and Malachy from the time in which the soldiers were squeezing their triggers. Then he sat up, smiling as the ropes which bound them untied themselves and fell to the ground.

Malachy stared at him. 'How is this possible?' he demanded.

'The moment at which those rifles are being fired is still taking place,' Dante told him, 'but I have removed us beyond its scope. Now, go! Quickly! Before my concentration lapses and the ticking of the world begins once more.'

THE MOST BEAUTIFUL VOICE

It had been hot and sultry all day, with rumblings of distant thunder and occasional flashes of lightning, but so far the storm had not broken. Bea, Seersha, Albigen and Eugenius arrived in Eden Valley late in the evening. Albigen led them to the deserted village in which the Púca had made their camp.

Everyone was overjoyed to see Bea. She was greeted with smiles and hugs. But, despite this, she could not help feeling something was missing. And when Ezekiel came to meet her she realised what it was. She recalled their first meeting after he had been wheeled back from the shock room on Tarnagar. Even strapped to the bed and labelled a madman, he had been certain of his power, confident in his judgement and unintimidated by authority. But now he seemed quite frail and she thought she detected a faint trembling as he took her hands.

'It's so wonderful to see you again,' she told him, but her words sounded hollow. It was as if she had thought she recognised an old friend in a crowd, but then realised, as she crossed the room to meet him, that she had been mistaken.

For a long time they stood face to face, his pale blue eyes looking straight into hers. At last he shook his head.

'There is something about you that I do not understand,' he said.

'Not something bad, I hope?' she replied.

'I don't know whether it is bad or good,' he told her. 'But it is imminent, that much I can tell.' He gave a wry smile and for a moment she was reminded of the old Ezekiel. 'I think you have become very important, little Bea,' he said.

Bea smiled uncertainly. 'I don't feel very important,' she told him.

'It is not how we think of ourselves that matters,' he replied gravely. 'It is what we do.'

Just then Maeve came running up and threw her arms around Bea. 'I thought I'd never see you again,' she said.

'You wouldn't have done, but for Dante.'

They were all anxious to hear about Dante. She told them about his visit to the museum and blushed as she described how she had set off the alarm. 'He would have been captured if Seersha hadn't helped him escape,' she added.

After the introductions and explanations were over, some of the Púca set about preparing a meal. 'It won't be very exciting,' Maeve told them. 'We have to live on whatever we can find. Tonight it's rabbit stew.'

They soon had a fire going and the air was full of the smell of cooking. It felt wonderful to be sitting round the fire in the open air, sharing a meal and conversation with old friends. And the stew, when it arrived, tasted delicious. The excitement of the day's events had made

Bea forget how hungry she was and for a little while she could think of nothing but eating. Only when she had finished every last morsel did she look up again.

'You must tell me everything that happened after the soldiers attacked Moiteera,' she began. 'The last thing I remember...' but before she could finish her sentence they were interrupted by a shout from the other end of the village.

'That's Ezekiel!' Albigen said, springing to his feet and rushing off in the direction of the cry. The others followed close at his heels.

They found Ezekiel standing at the edge of the village staring wildly in front of him. In one hand he held a burning stick which he was slowly waving back and forth. 'Don't come any closer!' he cried when he saw them.

'What is it?' Albigen shouted back.

'Sumaira. They live on blood,' Ezekiel replied. 'Look at them! They would have devoured us while we slept!' He continued to brandish the burning stick in front of him and yelled as if he was trying to scare off an animal.

'But where are they?' Maeve cried.

'What do you mean?' Ezekiel demanded angrily. 'They're right in front of me.' He swung the flaming torch in a wide circle.

Albigen, Maeve and Bea all looked at each other. 'We can't see anything,' Albigen said.

'They're everywhere!' Ezekiel told him. 'Look out! There's one right behind you.'

All three wheeled round but they could see nothing out of the ordinary.

'Perhaps they're invisible,' Maeve said.

'Perhaps, or perhaps there's nothing there,' Albigen replied, speaking softly so that Ezekiel could not hear him.

'I think they're leaving,' Ezekiel said. 'They're afraid of fire!' He was waving the torch around furiously now and making short runs back and forth as if he were driving away a whole herd of creatures. 'Go back to the Nakara where you belong!' he yelled. By now many more of the Púca had gathered to watch. Several of them shook their heads in bewilderment.

'I don't think we need to worry about them any more tonight,' Ezekiel said, coming back to join them at last. 'They prefer to go about their business in secret. They don't like light and noise. My god, though, they're filthy creatures. Look at the slime! It's everywhere.' He turned to Albigen. 'Is everyone all right?'

'Everyone's fine,' Albigen assured him.

'I want you to check on the cottages,' Ezekiel told him. 'Make sure there are no casualties.'

'Of course.'

Maeve went over to Ezekiel and put her hand on his arm. 'You need to rest now,' she told him.

'I can't afford to rest!' he replied. 'We don't know what else might appear before the night is over.'

'All the same,' Maeve said. 'We need you to be strong, Ezekiel. You have to conserve your energy.'

Reluctantly, he allowed her to lead him back to his cottage.

'I'll come with you to check on the village,' Bea told Albigen.

'We won't find anything,' Albigen replied.

'Are you sure?'

'This isn't the first time Ezekiel has driven off imaginary enemies.'

Bea looked at him. She had never heard anyone question Ezekiel's judgement before. 'Why are you so sure they're imaginary?' she asked.

'Because he's the only one who ever sees them.'

'How long has this been going on?'

'Ever since our last mission to sabotage an Ichor processing plant. Ezekiel discovered that our enemy is producing a new drug of some kind. He's convinced it opens up the depths of the Odyll and that all sorts of creatures have been coming out.'

'But perhaps it's true.'

'Perhaps,' Albigen conceded. 'But no one else can see any evidence of it. I'll tell you what I do see, though. Something bad is happening to Ezekiel. He's growing weaker all the time but he can't rest. It's as if he's being consumed from the inside.'

'Poor Ezekiel!'

'Yes. I don't know how much longer he can stand it. In the meantime the day to day leadership of the Púca is falling increasingly on my shoulders.'

'You're the best fighter among the Púca,' Bea told him. 'The others know that and they respect you.'

'Yes, but all I have is my strength,' Albigen replied. 'We need Ezekiel's powers. Without them we haven't got a chance.'

They continued their inspection of the village in

silence. At each of the cottages, they received the same answer: everything was all right, no one was harmed, no one had seen or heard any fearsome creatures.

'How much do you understand about the Odyll, Bea?' Albigen asked, when they had finished their tour.

'Not much.'

'Me too,' Albigen admitted, 'and to be honest, I'm not sure I want to. But not long after I first met him, Ezekiel told me that being aware of the Odyll is like living with a wild animal. As long as you're strong, it respects you and allows you to control it. But if you ever start to weaken, it will devour you without mercy.'

Bea shuddered. 'You talk as if it were alive.'

'That's what I said,' Albigen replied. 'Ezekiel looked at me like I was a fool and said, of course it's alive.'

They had reached the cottage that had been allocated to Bea and Seersha. 'You must be tired,' Albigen said. 'You should get some sleep.'

'Okay,' Bea agreed. 'But just tell me this. What do you think will happen to him?'

Albigen shrugged. 'I don't know. All I can tell you is what Ezekiel told me himself a few nights ago. He said that his time with us is nearly over.'

Bea looked at him in dismay. 'That can't be true!?'

'I think he's just hanging on in the hope that Dante will arrive.'

They said good night then and Bea went into her cottage. She found Seersha busy stacking the little collection of supplies they had taken from the back of the truck.

The cottage was very basic. There were two rooms downstairs: a kitchen and a living room. But there was no water in the taps nor anything to be found in the cupboards, except what Seersha had put there. Upstairs were two more rooms, but no beds. Bea didn't mind sleeping on the floor. Freedom was more important than comfort.

Since it was too early to sleep, Bea and Seersha sat downstairs in the living room propped up against the walls on either side, discussing the day's events. Outside, the storm grew nearer and the sky became darker. They lit a candle and watched the play of shadows against the wall.

'You know when we first drove out of the museum gates, I expected someone to...' Seersha began.

Bea turned to see why her friend had stopped in mid-sentence and saw that Seersha was sitting with her mouth open, staring directly in front of her.

'What is it?' Bea asked.

Then Bea noticed that the candle flame had halted in its dance and the shadows on the wall were still, the same deep stillness that had been all around her when Ezekiel Semiramis had led them out of Tarnagar. Instinctively, she understood that time had become infinitely slow. What was no more than a fraction of a second for Seersha was being stretched and expanded for her. And it was not happening by chance. An event of the profoundest importance was taking place.

Bea turned from Seersha and found that someone else was with her in the room. A young man with shoulder length hair, wearing a white robe that reached down to his ankles towered in front of her. Projecting from his shoulder blades were two enormous feathered wings.

The winged man opened his mouth and spoke. 'My name is Tzavinyah. I am the messenger of the Odyll,' he told her.

It was the most beautiful voice Bea had ever heard. The very sound of his name was like bells ringing out across a landscape of snow and ice. The coldness of that world swept over Bea so that she shivered. Then immediately she felt as if she were bathed in warm water so that she wanted to cry out with sheer pleasure.

'I bring news for the betrayer,' the winged man continued.

'Who is the betrayer?' she asked. Her voice sounded tiny and child-like.

'You are. Sorrow follows at your heels like night follows day. But do not spend time regretting it. Remember only this: upon the thread of your forgiveness hangs the fate of the world.'

Then the candle flickered, and he was gone. Seersha looked at Bea and frowned. 'What was I just saying?' she asked.

THE END OF THE HUNT

Ezekiel sat in his cottage with his head in his hands. He knew that the others did not believe him. And he was beginning to think they might be right. It was getting hard to tell the difference between his private fears and the dangers that threatened the very existence of the Púca.

As he was thinking this, the silence of the night was broken by the howling of wolves. Wearily, he got to his feet and went outside the cottage to investigate.

The howling came again, much nearer this time. Several other Púca came outside and looked anxiously about them.

Above them the sky was lit up by a violet streak of lightning and a moment later the rain began lashing down with astonishing force. And with the rain the wolves came, racing in from every corner of the village and hurling themselves upon the Púca.

Ezekiel tried to collect himself and reach into the odyllic world but all around him the men and women he loved were fighting for their lives against opponents that wanted more than anything to rip open their throats.

Suddenly, a human figure came running towards them at terrifying speed, snarling and gnashing his teeth, his eyes like those of an animal.

To Ezekiel's astonishment, the young man looked just like Dante. Yet from the expression on his face, it was clear that he was determined to attack them.

'Dante! What are you doing?' Ezekiel shouted. But his words fell on deaf ears. His attacker threw himself forwards, flinging his fist in Ezekiel's face and driving his knee upwards towards his groin. Ezekiel side-stepped and tried to get him in a neck lock but the young man wriggled out with contemptuous ease and flew at him.

Ezekiel struggled as furiously as he had ever done in his life. His opponent seemed to feel no pain. Again and again, Ezekiel threw the young man to the ground, but he kept coming back, to kick, claw and bite. And now his hands pressed around Ezekiel's throat.

Little by little, Ezekiel felt himself being steadily overpowered. Summoning up all his strength for one last effort, he broke free of his opponent's grip and hurled him backwards. The young man struck his head against a rock and lay still.

Ezekiel breathed a sigh of relief and turned to see Maeve and Bea backed up against the wall of a hut by a wolf. Maeve had picked up a broken tree branch and was brandishing it in the animal's direction, but it leapt at her and tore the branch from her grasp. Ezekiel was just bracing himself to leap at the wolf when he heard Bea shouting at him to look out. He turned and saw that his attacker was back on his feet.

Deep within himself he knew that he could not

withstand another onslaught. But he had to try! His feelings must have shown, for a smile spread slowly across the young man's face.

What came next happened so quickly that there was no time for Bea to waiver. She did not fully understand what was happening but she was certain of this much: the person who was attacking Ezekiel was not Dante. The resemblance was extraordinary but it was like looking at Dante's reflection in a cracked mirror. And if she did not stop him, this hideous forgery of her friend would kill Ezekiel.

Leaving Maeve to handle the wolf, she took the kitchen knife from her pocket. Calling upon all the hours she had spent training for such an occasion, she raised it above her head and ran.

But, like an eel, the young man twisted to one side and his arm snaked out, seizing her hand. At the same time his head came down and his jaws locked onto her arm, biting down with so much force that she screamed and her fingers released their grip. Immediately, he grabbed the knife and turned in one movement, throwing himself once more upon Ezekiel. Ezekiel put out his arms to defend himself – but the knife buried itself deep within his heart.

THE QUARRY

Gallowglass felt nothing at the death of his opponent. Neither triumph nor regret. The man had fought well, much better than he had expected, but now he was defeated and the only thing that mattered was the girl. Her capture was his sole purpose and he would not allow himself to become distracted by any other matter.

She stood like a statue, horror and anguish written across her face, so busy blaming herself for what had happened that she had no strength left to resist. It was a simple matter to seize her round the throat and pin her arm behind her back. She screamed with pain but the voice of the thunder covered up her cries and the wolves held her companions at bay while he dragged her away into the darkness.

Before the attack, Gallowglass had surveyed the territory thoroughly, familiarising himself with every feature of the landscape. He had memorised the route, taking note of any obstacles it might present, so that even the violence of the storm did not confuse him. He dragged the girl away as quickly as he could but now that she was away from the site of her companion's death, her senses returned to her and she kicked and fought with all her strength. He thought, just for a moment, he might lose his grip. Angrily, he pushed her arm further up her back and squeezed the breath out of her throat until she stopped struggling and he could continue to carry her unimpeded.

Not far from the holiday village was an abandoned quarry where ancient diggings had cut away a great swathe of the land. This was his destination. But the torrential rain was turning the ground into a sea of mud and he slipped and slithered as he went. More than once he lost his footing completely, taking the girl down with him. Yet each time he rose again, pulled the girl to her feet and pressed on.

Everything depended on the Master. Gallowglass had no plans for the girl himself. He was neither cruel nor merciful. Such considerations were unnecessary. When lightning hits a tree, it feels no pity for the branch that is burnt, nor does it rejoice that the wood has turned to ash. It merely acts according to its nature. And it was his nature to carry out his Master's orders – swiftly, effectively and without question.

At last they reached the top of the hill, and now the quarry was not far away. Desperately, the girl tried to reason with him. 'Why are you doing this?' she asked. 'Where are you taking me? Please just stop for a minute! Listen to me. My name is Bea. I'm a person like you. You have to understand that what you're doing is wrong.' Over and over again she repeated the same empty words.

Gallowglass did his best to ignore her. She was just like all the others – trusting to speech when she should have relied on strength and singleness of purpose. Nevertheless, he felt her words clinging to him and slowing him down like the mud that already coated them both.

'Quiet!' he shouted but she carried on regardless, begging him to let her go, promising to help him if he did so, though what help she could possibly offer, he could not imagine.

That was the trouble with human beings, the thing that made them so weak, this business of endlessly debating every action, looking at the choices involved and asking yourself whether they were good or bad. Gallowglass wanted to tell her this. But to do so would draw him into the ridiculous dance of language. And besides, he needed all his strength to drag her along because she continued to snatch at every tree or bush to slow them down.

Then, just within sight of the quarry's edge, he slipped in the mud once more, and released his hold. Much more quickly than he had expected, she raced away from him into the night. He was furious with himself. It was her ridiculous words that had caused this! He sprang to his feet and gave chase and though she managed to evade him briefly, it was not long before he threw himself upon her.

With a cry of dismay she crumpled beneath him. Quickly he stood up and pulled her to her feet. When she stared defiantly back at him, he struck her as hard as he could across the face with the flat of his hand. She staggered backwards under the blow. Then he seized her by the throat once more and dragged her back up the hill.

Now she simply stumbled along beside him, waiting to find out his intentions. So it was that Gallowglass reached the very lip of the quarry and peered over the edge at the sheer drop on the other side and the dark water that swirled at its base. Now he had only to wait for the Master to make his decision.

THE CHOICE

For the last two hours Dante and Malachy had been travelling above the storm, looking down on a thick blanket of cloud. It made flying easier but it meant that it was impossible to tell where they were. 'We'll have to go lower,' Malachy shouted, and Dante nodded. In preparation, he set about creating a bubble of odyllic force around the plane. Though this required a huge effort of concentration, he delighted in his new powers.

When he was satisfied that they were protected from the wind and rain, he allowed Malachy to turn the nose of the plane downwards. As they descended into the very heart of the storm, Dante began searching the ground for the Púca's hideout. On the day he had left Moiteera to take Bea to hospital, Ezekiel had given him directions. Forty miles to the west of Moiteera was the town of Vendas and ten miles to the north of Vendas was a deserted holiday village. That was where the Púca would make their camp.

At last he saw a cluster of lights and buildings that had to be Vendas. 'There it is!' he called out to Malachy. 'Fly due north of that town and keep low.'

But the holiday village was not easy to find. It had been built to blend in with the countryside and years of neglect had allowed nature to throw a net of camouflage over the place. In the violence of the storm, they might have missed it completely, had not Malachy spotted the tell-tale pin-pricks of light in an ocean of darkness. They flew lower to investigate but suddenly Dante felt himself rocked by a huge surge of energy, as if the plane had been struck by lightning.

'What was that?' he yelled when he had recovered his wits.

'What was what?' Malachy shouted back.

'Didn't you feel anything just then?'

Malachy shook his head and Dante realised that the disturbance had been in the odyllic world. To understand what had caused it he would have to remove his attention from protecting the plane. Reluctantly, he did so and immediately the full force of the storm was unleashed upon them.

'What the hell's going on?' Malachy shouted.

But Dante was too busy concentrating on the last echoes of that bewildering explosion. Already the shockwaves were dying away but as he focused his mind on what was left, he suddenly understood the reason for it – something had happened to Ezekiel.

'Find somewhere to land!' he ordered Malachy. 'Hurry, please!'

'Easy for you to say,' Malachy called back. Still struggling against the fury of the storm, he circled over the area twice, shaking his head. Finally, he called out, 'I'm going to have to bring it down in the middle of the village. There's no other option.'

As they got lower, Dante could see some sort of struggle was taking place down below, but it was almost impossible to tell what was really happening. He wished desperately that he was on the ground to help.

'Here we go!' Malachy shouted, steering the plane between the lines of cottages. Dante could see people scattering in all directions. And could those be wolves running off into the darkness?

The wheels of the plane made contact with the road and they bounced along alarmingly, crashing through a wooden fence before finally grinding to a halt.

Malachy was bleeding where he had hit his mouth on the throttle and Dante felt badly bruised all over. But he scrambled rapidly from the plane and ran back towards the village. Amid the darkness and rain, everything was chaos and it was clear that a number of the Púca were seriously wounded. He ran over to a group gathered around a figure lying on the ground. As he got closer, he saw Maeve's father, Manachee.

'Dante?' Manachee said in amazement. 'Is it really you?'

'Of course it's me,' Dante said impatiently. 'Where's Ezekiel?'

Manachee sighed. 'Ezekiel is dead.'

'But I was sent here to save his life.'

'Then you arrived too late. That's him, on the ground over there.'

Dante bent down over Ezekiel's body. A dark pool of blood had formed on the ground around him. 'Ezekiel, it's me,' he said. 'Tzavinyah sent me to help you. I'm sorry I got here so late. Listen to me, Ezekiel, please.

You can't leave us. We need you. You're our leader. Please wake up. Please.'

He felt someone touch him on the shoulder and looked up.

'He's gone,' Manachee told him.

At these words, hope drained out of Dante and he remembered what Tzavinyah had told him – that the past cannot be changed. 'I'm sorry, Ezekiel,' he said. 'I failed you.' He got to his feet and walked away, tears blurring his eyes.

A little way away, Malachy had stopped and was staring in disbelief at a woman who sat with her back against a wall and her head in her hands. Slowly, he walked over to her. 'Seersha,' he said quietly. 'Is that really you?'

She looked up at him and her eyes widened in amazement. 'Malachy!' she cried, jumping to her feet. Then they wrapped their arms around each other and stood there in silence, the only two people to have found happiness on that dreadful night.

'Dante!' a voice called out.

Dante looked up and saw Maeve running towards him. Her clothes were torn and there was blood on her face but otherwise she seemed unharmed. 'I knew it wasn't you!' she said. 'Listen, we have to help Bea!' she told him.

Dante shook his head. 'Bea is in Barzach,' he told her bitterly. 'She remembers nothing.'

'No she's not!' Maeve insisted. 'She arrived here this evening but she was dragged off by the young man who led the attack. Dante, there's something you should know. He looks just like you!'

Dante stared at her in confusion. He could not make sense of what she was trying to tell him but he was determined that Bea would not meet the same fate as Ezekiel. 'I'll get her back, Maeve,' he promised. 'And I'll make him pay for what he's done, I swear it.'

'I'll come with you,' Maeve volunteered.

'No. You stay here and look after the people who are hurt. I can handle this by myself.' The truth was, he didn't want anyone to come with him. This was personal, between him and Ezekiel's killer. The desire for revenge burned within him.

He reached into the Odyll and was immediately aware of the killer's trail. Whoever had made it was filled with so much negative energy that it had overflowed from him, leaving a stain in the Odyllic world like the marks of filthy boots on a newly washed floor. Dante sprang forward in pursuit.

On the edge of the cliff, with death only moments away, Bea suddenly had the strangest feeling. She was no longer afraid. What was more, her former fear and anxiety seemed to have transferred itself to her attacker. Even in the darkness she could see how his face continually twitched and how he swallowed compulsively. He was not much older than herself, she realised, and there was obviously something terribly wrong with him. She thought about the way he had fought Ezekiel, like an animal, as if he had forgotten what it meant to be human. She saw too how he stared out into the darkness as though waiting for a sign, and it began to dawn on her that he had lost control of his mind, that someone else was controlling every move he made.

'Whoever it is, you don't have to obey,' she said.

He looked at her in astonishment.

'You have a choice, you know,' she went on. 'What you did back there was wrong but someone else was directing you, weren't they? You can take back control of your life. It's up to you, all of it.'

A look of pain passed across the young man's face and for a moment she thought he was going to speak. But then a figure appeared running up the hill towards them. And this time she knew without a shadow of a doubt that it was Dante. He was surrounded by a pale blue light and was so obviously full of power that even Bea found she was frightened of him. At the same time an old man seemed to materialise out of nowhere. He was standing only a short distance away from her and all around him were tall purple flowers. At first she could not place him. Then she realised that it was Doctor Sigmundus.

Dante stopped and looked from Sigmundus to Bea's captor, and back again.

'Well, Dante Cazabon,' Sigmundus began. 'As you see, you must tread very carefully now, for I have only to give the command and your little friend Beatrice will plunge to her death. Alternatively, I can order my servant to release her. But for that to happen you must open your mind to me.'

Dante's eyes blazed and he shook his head. 'Your threat means nothing,' he replied. 'This murdering beast will not harm Bea because I will not allow it.' He raised his hand and Bea fully expected a bolt of energy to fly from the end of it.

'Wait!' Sigmundus ordered. 'Perhaps you should think twice before you kill your own brother.'

Dante's arm dropped to his side. 'My brother?' he whispered.

'It is true,' Sigmundus went on, 'though I have to confess, it was only by good fortune that I encountered him myself. He stumbled upon a little experiment I was conducting. And, unlike all my other subjects, he was an immediate success. That was what made me investigate him more closely. It seems your mother was smuggled into Tavor to give birth. And our friend here was stolen by one of the nurses who could not have a child of her own. She brought him up to believe he was her son – but I found out the truth. So now it's up to you, Dante. Will you kill your own brother?'

Dante stood in silence. All the determination had left his face. Instead he looked utterly helpless. A cruel smile crossed the old man's face. Then he opened his mouth but this time it was not the voice of Sigmundus that spoke. Instead, Dante heard dozens of different voices, pleading, whining and threatening all at the same time. But each one spoke the same words: 'Let me in!'

Dante had no doubt about what he was hearing. These were the voices of all those whom Orobas had absorbed over the centuries. And the moment he surrendered, he would become like them, a part of the creature's collective identity.

It was Gallowglass who broke the silence. He put his hands on his head and screamed, a sound that was neither completely human nor animal. Then he stepped forward and fell headlong over the cliff into the dark water below.

Sigmundus staggered as if he has been dealt a physical blow. Dante, however, was like someone released from a spell. A wave of fury overtook him as he thought of how the deaths of Ezekiel and of this poor, twisted creature had been caused by nothing more than vanity, a lust for power and a desire for life prolonged beyond its natural span.

The power of the Odyll surged through him with such force that he thought it might wash him away like a mighty river. But then, channelling its strength into a single stream of energy, he pointed his finger once more at the body of Doctor Sigmundus.

'Your time is finished,' he said and a bolt of power burst from him. With a scream, the old man flew backwards through the air, landing spread-eagled on the ground some distance away, utterly motionless.

Cautiously, Dante advanced towards the body, his lip curled in disgust. Sigmundus was dead and with him Orobas, the creature that had inhabited his body. Dante rejoiced, feeling nothing but hatred for his opponent and pleasure at the vengeance he had delivered.

He crouched down over the body, determined to make sure that the job had been done properly. Sigmundus's eyes were closed. His breathing had stopped. Dante let out a long sigh of relief. Then he stood up and spat upon the ground.

He turned to walk away – but in that instant Sigmundus's eyes opened. His lips curved upwards in a twisted smile.

'I thank you for your hatred, Dante Cazabon,' said a voice.

Dante spun around.

'It was all the invitation I needed.'

Dante opened his mouth to reply but instead his whole body shuddered and twisted spasmodically. His mind was filled with a thousand voices shouting and laughing gleefully. Transfixed with horror, he felt his true self shrinking and diminishing as the creature from the depths of the Odyll took possession of his body.

EPILOGUE

The storm that had battered Gehenna was over. Beside a disused quarry in a valley not far from the little town of Vendas, an old man lay on the ground. Beside him a youth stood utterly motionless, hands raised to his head in a despairing gesture, a look of shock and horror written across his face. On the very edge of the nearby cliff a girl stared at them both in dismay.

Unnoticed, a small bird flew down and landed on the ground nearby. It opened its beak and its tiny call disturbed the silence.

The old man's eyelids fluttered briefly, then closed as the life went out of his body completely. Immediately, the youth beside him let out a piercing cry of anguish.

The bird rose into the air and flew rapidly away, its tiny form silhouetted against the growing darkness. Night was coming to Tavor and to Gehenna. In time, its shadow would spread across the whole world and embrace every living thing – for the appetite of Orobas knew no bounds.

OTHER ORCHARD BOOKS YOU MAY ENJOY

ALL PRICED AT £5.99

Orchard books are available from all good bookshops, or can be ordered direct from the publisher: Orchard Books, PO BOX 29, Douglas IM99 1BQ
Credit card orders please telephone 01624 836000
or fax 01624 837033 or visit our website: www.orchardbooks.co.uk
or e-mail: bookshop@enterprise.net for details.

To order please quote title, author and ISBN
and your full name and address.
Cheques and postal orders should be made payable to 'Bookpost plc.'
Postage and packing is FREE within the UK
(overseas customers should add £1.00 per book).

Prices and availability are subject to change.